YOU ARE A BIRD

BREEZY VAN LIT

SHIMMER TREE BOOKS

YOU ARE A BIRD

Shimmer Tree Books

Print ISBN: 979-8-9864145-0-8

Published by Shimmer Tree Books, Shimmer Tree LLC

This book is dedicated to you.

YOU

ARE

A BIRD

1

Cage

You are a bird in a cage.

You don't remember ever not being a bird. Isn't that how it is for everyone?

But the cage. It's not that you can recall a time outside of it. It's more of a sense. Like many things of that nature, this sense comes and goes like the breeze, or at least like you imagine the breeze might be if you could experience it directly. Instead, you look out of the window, a muddled pane, and you see a single blurry shrub forever drifting south on the ledge of an enormous rock, pushed by an invisible force you do not feel.

Were you ever out there? Outside? Were you on the ground, afraid, and the next thing you knew, you were in this cage?

There's no way to be sure. What you know are poles of wood, crisscrossing and bent into a globular enclosure. All utility and no soul. Your home.

But you don't want this to be understood as complaining. The water's always semi-clean. You're never without food, however dry and unvarying it might be. A high percentage of your waste is cleaned out from the bottom of the cage by Man. It could be roomier, yet it does have, not one, but two perches. You sense that resting on the bough of a living tree would be better than clinging to this dowel, wood from a dead tree, but would it be?

This thought, like so many, is vague and bendy.

2

Puzzle

Man chatters on at you.

You wonder if he is chirping, but his tone is so deep. It doesn't carry a melody with it like yours does.

His huge hand enters your cage closed in a fist. It's big enough to pound down on you and end your life. Instead, it releases a mixture of seeds and grains into a ceramic dish and gives you a long pat on the head.

You chirp back a soft collection of notes, almost a coo.

He fills the air with his booming sounds, and his hand leaves the cage. Closes the door.

He pulls a thin sheet of wood so a portion of it hangs off the edge of a table and twists the handle of a device that clamps it into place.

You hop from your lower perch to the upper perch, which takes just a few wing flaps to accomplish. From up here, you can see that Man's sheet of wood has elaborate markings on it.

He picks up a saw with a thin blade and begins cutting into the wood. Slow and precise, he works the blade through the picture in smooth curves.

Kaz told you before, Man's a puzzle maker, but that doesn't make sense. Why would someone paint a picture, and quite a well-done picture at that, and then dissect it into pieces for someone else to put back together?

"Humans think it's fun," Kaz says.

"Was I thinking out loud again?" you say.

"No, thoughts are immaterial. You were speaking out loud."

You prevent your next thoughts from manifesting into speech.

You'd rather have Kaz around than not, even if the cat does have a hungry look in his eyes now and then, but you could do without his opinions on this matter. He often misses the deeper point, though he's a world better than Fay.

Fay is too much like you. Swimming around her bowl.

A fish in her bowl; a bird in your cage.

That said, at least she swims. You can't really call flitting between two perches flying.

3

Glass

Man picks up the wooden box, now filled with the separated pieces of his picture. He walks out of the door, Kaz slinking beside him nearly attached to his leg. The cat's tail waves gaily as if to taunt you. You think Man might stop to say goodbye, but he does not.

∞

You like the way the fire looks, its silky light licking upward through Fay's fishbowl. It flickers on the wall behind you in a faint impression of its origin in the hearth. Kaz has told you it could burn or even kill you. But how could that be? How could something so beautiful hurt you?

"Does that fire warm your water?" you ask Fay.

"What water?" she says.

This is where conversations with Fay always get frustrating. "The water you're swimming in." You're proud of yourself for hiding even a hint of condescension in your tone.

"Don't know what you're talking about, bird. Also, to be clear, I'm not swimming at the moment. I'd call this floating."

"And you're floating in?" you say, trying to help Fay along.

"Just floating. Same as you."

"I'm sitting on a piece of wood, surrounded by air."

"Air?"

"It's like the water you're in . . . but not wet . . . and thinner . . . much thinner." You regret trying to explain to her something you do not have the words for yourself.

"Right." Fay gives you that look. There's nothing more deflating than being smirked at by a fish.

"Well, there are things that exist in the world that you can't see," you say.

"Like what?"

"The air in my cage. The water in your bowl." Fay's blank stare gets you fluttered, which propels you to your upper perch. "And . . . truth!"

"What is truth?"

"It's true that you're in water, and the water is surrounded by glass!"

"Glass?"

Your wings shoot down to your sides. "I can prove it to you. Swim toward me." You consider adding the word "quickly" but decide that would be too mean. "Slowly, Fay."

Fay wiggles her fins. She passes over large grains of sand, around the tendrils of a wispy plant, through a tunnel in a rock, and comes to a sudden stop as she bumps into the glass of her bowl. She scrunches her face.

"That is glass," you say.

Fay shakes her head. "No. That's the edge of the world."

"What about me?" you say, not hiding your exasperation. "How can I be out here then?"

"You're in your world. I'm in my world. And never the twain shall meet. It's all relative, bird."

Fay is a fish who doesn't know she's in water talking to a bird who knows you are in a cage.

4

Psyche

Man walks into the room, Kaz in tow, and places a couple of items on his desk. He picks up a picture from the top of the stack, looks at it, smiling, and tacks it to the wooden wall.

You don't know why the picture pleases him. It's nothing like his paintings he cuts into pieces, exquisite in their detail. This drawing is in one waxy color, blue. It is a swirling vision, sort of like the water and sand in Fay's bowl when she swims in tight circles.

Next, he opens the drawer, takes out a knife, and rips into the top of an envelope. Reading the letter inside, he lets out a snuff of air.

Kaz curls up in front of the fire while Man approaches a chessboard arranged atop a pedestal. He sits on a stool, looks up from the letter in his hand, and moves a light-stained piece from the opposite side of the board toward himself.

His face becomes small as he stares at the board. Tugs at the edges of his oversized mustache, which crests the brown and white whiskers of his overflowing beard.

"He looks so foolish when he does that," you say.

"He looks foolish planning his next move in this game," Kaz says, "but you do not look foolish watching him planning his next move? In judgment, no less?"

Kaz's purred words burn into you. You hop to your lower perch. Man looks up and smiles, presumably seeing your activity as an expression of playfulness. But it's not. It is a descent. One step removed from the septic platform below.

Man returns to his desk and picks up a mysterious object. It reflects the glare from the window at one angle and the flame of the fire from another. He crosses the narrow space to you, reaches in your cage, and places the object so it sits above your dish.

You look inside and see a bird!

Oh, glorious day! You appreciate Man and Kaz and even Fay, but a bird—one of you. Someone who relates to you, with whom you can share thoughts that Man can't fathom and the other two don't care about.

You hop from perch to perch, chirping your gratitude to Man and words of welcome to your guest.

Man lets out a great baritone howl, which, given the expression accompanying it on his face, you interpret as a laugh—a joyful laugh. Kaz shakes his head. Fay sloshes around her tank, stirred by your excitement, to the point that a splash of water escapes her world and lands on the floor of the world outside of her bowl.

As interesting as that would normally be, nothing compares to the magical moment happening in your cage. The arrival of one who could become a friend. Think of that. A friend.

A flash of paranoia. Is Man replacing you? Could this bird attack? It hasn't yet. Perish the thought.

Could it be a mate? Another thing you don't understand, but you sense. You can't detect any clues from this bird as to whether that is even a possibility; it seems to have no scent. In fact, looking down, the bird has disappeared! In its place, a vertical version of the horizontal floor of your cage. What?

You blast out a flurry of tweets.

No response.

"Bird," Kaz says, with an exaggerated grin on his face, "you should know . . ."

You ignore him. Not now. This is too important.

You hop to your lower perch to investigate. You look, and there is the bird again.

Well, this is odd.

You move in close. And it does, too. You shift your head to the right, then to the left. So does the bird. "Alright, it can't match this move," you say, eliciting a snicker from Kaz. You do a quick spin, your feet temporarily leaving your perch, touching down halfway around, and releasing again for the completion of your revolution.

You can't see the bird while you spin, of course, but it lands as you land.

And it's on a perch, too. But where is that perch? Your cage only has the two. You look up to be sure you aren't going crazy. There's one above you, the one you're on, and then . . . a third?

You lean in. And the bird leans in. You touch its beak, it taps yours. And you see that it is trapped in some flat, silvery dimension.

You look into its eyes, and you realize that you look into some manifestation of your own. Deeper in. All space, no essence.

You have been duped.

5

Feathers

Whirling stars clicking into one another over streams of satin ribbon. That's how you would describe the sounds you hear.

However much you try to ignore it, you cannot.

You are a musical being, constructed with a connection to rhythms and notes that communicate more clearly than words, more powerfully than pleasure or pain.

Man cranks a handle, which spins a wheel; taps his fingers on buttons pressing into wood. And the melody flows.

Kaz says the instrument is called a hurdy-gurdy. You question whether Kaz is being serious. Hurdy-gurdy? Humans are strange creatures, but that just sounds absurd.

The music the hurdy-gurdy produces is not absurd. It makes you wonder if Man is a god.

Eyes closed, breathing through his nose, Man's hand cycles and fingers dance. And from his machine, those celestial sparks ascend and descend a spiral tower in your mind.

The melody torments you. Not because it is harsh or hideous, but because it is arresting in its beauty. The notes fly. And that makes you sense that you should fly. That you must fly.

But that is not possible.

Wood surrounds you.

The curving bars of your cage and the straight perch to which you cling. The creaky floorboards below Man's foot, which he taps to the crescendoing tempo of his music, and above which Kaz's tail sways. The wood of the mantle and the walls composing the room enclosing your cage. The ceiling, in thick, impenetrable beams. The wooden desk and chair. Chessboard and its pieces, pedestal, and stool. Bookshelf filled with books filled with paper. Easel and the wood sheet it displays—blank now, but soon to be covered with paint and cut into pieces. And as the pieces separate, the dust that falls from the saw blade—wood.

Dead wood.

Kaz claims there is living wood outside of this room, and lots of it. He says the image you see through the window on the rock is a twig compared to the forest of living wood he has roamed—which is not, in fact, far from where you perch.

The closest thing to living wood in your presence is the magic box Man twists and taps, making it breathe its wordless song of unattainable hope.

You sink so low your beak bumps into your chest. When you lift it, you discover within its grasp a plucked feather.

∞

Blue swirls, sprinkles of green, a splotch of brown on the surface of a light grain of wood.

Man looks at an unfurled paper on his table, the worn edges held in place by little jars of paint, then back to his easel.

He guides his paintbrush to give shape to the colors. You've watched him paint a picture of you before. One of Fay. Several of Kaz. Mountains, castles, gardens. And many others. All of which were eventually separated into puzzles and placed into boxes. But you can't make this one out.

You ask Kaz, who at the moment is much more entertained by the erratic pattern Fay cuts through the water in her bowl.

His tail stops flicking back and forth as he looks over his shoulder at the painting. "It's a map."

"What's a map?" you ask.

"It's a representation of how the land and the water of an area are arranged."

Kaz looks at you with pity, knowing your understanding about what takes place outside of this room comes only from his descriptions—not that he often goes out of his way to educate you unless you make a request.

"It's like the picture he painted of you, the one you were excited about until you saw him cut it into a puzzle," Kaz continued. "That painting represented you. Well, there's a whole world out there, and Man is painting a small picture of what that big world looks like."

"Are there giants at the corners of the world?" you say. "With wings?"

Kaz walks closer to Man and his painting. "Those are angels."

With a few swishes of his paintbrush, Man makes curling wisps flow out of their mouths.

Kaz raises his head and looks at you in your cage. "I believe their depiction symbolizes the idea that, though man has mapped the Earth, there is still a force beyond his control. The angels on the map suggest a benevolent source of that force."

Mammals are as baffling as they are intelligent.

"Are they real? Angels?"

"Winged creatures are your territory, bird."

"Well, I've never seen an angel," says Fay.

"All you've seen is what is physically present in this room," you reply.

"Exactly," she says as Kaz returns to watch her swim.

∞

Man adds gray triangles over a section of purple paint.

Your mind wanders to the window, and you try to imagine what is outside, the real land and water—the real world—that the map portrays.

Man regains your attention as he moves aside and stares at the paper on the table, which, from your upper perch, you can see is itself a model of what he paints.

Back to work at his easel.

You watch his hands. The hands that feed you and bring you water. Wrinkles of featherless flesh splattered with multi-colored dots and smears of paint. Calloused and tipped with rough fingernails.

One hand holds a palette of colorful paints while the other conjures objects on the sheet of wood. From flat blue, his movements draw forth white-capped waves and mysterious animals. Or are they monsters? And vessels sailing upon its surface.

The pictures he makes are intriguing, but then you look to the water in Fay's bowl and consider how the painting's sea conveys nothing of the liquid miracle that sloshes about in her "world."

You think back to the painting of you. Yes, you were excited when you saw it, as Kaz said. But only because of its novelty—you had never before seen your face, other than one fraction of it at a time in a transparent reflection in your water bowl.

Considering it now, like the painted water compared to real water, it must have been a poor likeness of you—even less impressive than the one appearing in the cursed reflective pane Man put in your cage. Kaz calls it a mirror. Whatever it is, you hate it.

And if the map, growing in spectacular detail before your eyes, is a mere whisper of the grand world beyond this space, then it too might as well be chopped into pieces and sent away in a box.

You reach down with your beak and pluck a feather from your chest. You spit it outside of your cage and watch it float to the floor.

6

Moonlight Aria

Kaz wandered out of the room hours ago, you assume to lounge in some other part of what he calls the "manor."

Man usually paints during the day, but he continues working on this one past nightfall by the light of an oil lamp.

He adds new elements and colors and curious markings. Kaz has told you that these markings are words—a collection of scribbles representing yet something else in the world.

You wonder why Man, who has access to the world beyond what you can see, spends so much time in this cell creating symbols that represent that world.

He dips his brushes in a jar of discolored water, puts his palette aside, and leaves the room. Returns with a roll and a glass containing a dark red liquid.

After taking a bite of bread, he breaks off a small piece and passes it through the cage to you.

You take it, and when he turns, even though it is topped with those little seeds you like, you release it from your beak. It lands among recently excreted waste.

Man looks to the painting, to the map on his table, and back to the painting. A big swig of his drink.

He puts his glass down with a crack. A drop of the liquid escapes the glass and splashes on the paper map. Man wipes it with his finger, which he then pops in his mouth as he approaches the chessboard. He moves a dark piece across several spaces of alternating shades of wood and places it on a light square.

He exhales a pleased huff of air and walks to his desk, where he removes a piece of paper from a drawer. Dark marks wiggle from the tip of his pen, dipped every few scrawls into an inkwell. More words you assume. His rough hands fold the paper into three parts with care and slide it into the opening of an envelope.

Another swig of his drink. His cheeks turn pink and he smiles, his eyes lifting to the drawing pinned on the wall.

He picks up a box from the top of the bookshelf. One of his projects. You don't think it will be a puzzle, but you don't know what it is.

He takes out a long, thin piece of wood and proceeds to shave and shape it with a folding knife. Thinner and thinner, with a slight twist along its surface.

You watch the tiniest threads of wood curl at the edge of the blade before falling to the tabletop and to the floor.

Man whistles a happy but meandering tune. You feel embarrassed listening. His pitches wander in and out, mostly out, of key, and the melody fails to make a point. It has little theme and no resolve. It does not say anything, at least, not to you. Maybe other humans would find it satisfying or helpful.

A new log on the fire. A bite of bread. A sip of drink. Pushing his blade across a new piece of wood that looks like the first. And so goes his work on into the night.

The last log burns down to a porous, gray shell with patches of smoldering orange. Man obliterates the gray shell with a poker and spreads the ash until the light is extinguished.

He picks up his empty glass, walks to the door, and stops with a grunt. Back to the table, to the still-burning oil lamp. He turns a knob, lowering the wick, cups his hand around the lamp's chimney, and blows a puff of air inside.

The flame out, he now leaves the room.

It's not total darkness. The window shimmers in soft silver. It must be the moon Kaz told you about.

A gigantic sphere floating in the sky? Circling the Earth?

You watched Kaz play with a ball of yarn before. It's the one time you've seen him not look distinguished. He batted it around for several minutes, propelling it across the room, pretending to sneak up on it—though it had been he himself who sent it scurrying across the floor in the first place.

When his jaws opened to attack it, you observed an arch of teeth, jagged protrusions accompanied by whiskers lunging forward in a menacing state of arousal.

He shot a few embarrassed glares at you and Fay— and at Man, who was howling in laughter at the whole episode—but he couldn't seem to stop his battle with the yarn.

You wondered if he would bat you around if you were down on that floor. He later said he wouldn't, but he wasn't very convincing. Even so, watching him play with that yarn in abandon led you to like him more for some reason.

You thought he might have made up the moon—his enchantment with the yarn getting the best of his imagination, or something like that. But then you saw Man add a luminous ball to the night sky in one of his paintings a few months later.

And now you watch its indirect glow in your blurry window.

You don't realize it for several bars, but you're whistling a tune. Two notes up, one note back. Two more notes up, one note back, along some scale planted into your soul without your knowing how or by whom.

The melody drops down, tapping a cooing rhythm into the air that bounces off the walls and back to you in a silky echo. Then soars up to a series of high notes capped in a trill.

Kaz doesn't like it when you whistle. He says your song is melancholy. Minor key. You only know the song you know. And from your cage, it is the song you sing.

Kaz isn't here to complain anyway. And Fay likes your music. She says it wobbles into her ears in quite a pleasing fashion.

So you whistle, on and on, as the silver window warms to gold.

7

Visitation

A bird in your cage.

But it's not you.

You launch to your upper perch. He's farther from you now, but you feel like you're closer than you were before you jumped away. Your perspective of him is universal in an odd way.

He looks at you. You sense that you can see a more complete you through his gaze.

Turns his head, back to work.

He presses his face as far as it will go between two bars of the cage and drags the sharp edge of his beak against something around the outside of the cage door. Kaz has described that area to you before as a fastener that holds the door in place.

Is he scraping the fastener?

You can't hear it. In fact, you can't hear anything. You whistle as a test. You can feel air flowing from your beak, but there is no sound. Just a subtle vibration within your own head.

Strange.

And you can feel the scraping. From the outer face of the door, across the arcing poles of the cage, through the perch, into your feet. And that sensation sends a chill through your body. A bad chill. A shiver of deep discomfort in which you sense the friction arising from the caustic contact between the bird's beak and the fastener.

He looks at you again.

Your eyes focus on the white scratches across the surface of his beak—deep, permanent.

And as quickly as he looks at you, he turns and is at it again, attacking the outside of the cage.

Though he is in the cage with you, he transcends the cage. Like he is both inside and outside of the cage at once. A paradox with wings.

Your thoughts mush into each other . . .

What happened to the sounds you should be hearing?

Did the bird come from the map? No, that doesn't make sense.

How did he get in the cage? From the mirror? Absurd. Maybe you're the one in the mirror, and he's the real bird?

If only Kaz were here.

You look through the window, usually foggy but now clear, and Kaz is there looking back at you, shaking his head side-to-side. The tree on the rock, always chasing the breeze, is still. And you can see it in vivid detail, down to the grain in the branches and the veins in the leaves.

You should check with Fay. Not a deep thinker, but possibly a good viewpoint given the circumstances. Is she experiencing what you're experiencing?

You spin on your perch and see her floating above the water of her bowl, on her back, fins behind her head. She winks at you and erupts into laughter, at least you assume it's laughter, though she doesn't make a sound.

∞

"Do cats dream?" you say to Kaz.

"Why do you ask?"

"I had a dream last night."

Kaz rolls over, away from you so he faces the fire.

You've noticed his attention drift before when you've shared a dream, but this one is too sticky to not explore.

"You were in my dream."

"I'm bigger in my dreams. Much bigger," Kaz says, moving his head to look at you over his shoulder. "Was I many times larger than I am now in your dream?"

"No. Regular size Kaz." You hop to your upper perch. "You were outside of the window."

"That window is on the second story of the manor. There's a ledge outside, but it's much too narrow for me."

"Well, the fact that you were out there was the least of the strangeness. There was a bird in my cage—"

"Not that strange. There's a bird in your cage now."

"You know what I mean—another bird, in addition to me."

"I've told you before, that is a mirror."

"No, it wasn't that. I don't even think the mirror was in the dream at all. The bird seemed to be picking and scraping at the fastener," you say, motioning to your cage door with your head.

"Dreams are meaningless," says Kaz. "A random assortment of memories and abstractions projecting onto the screen of the mind before draining out of the brain to make room for new information." He pauses as he turns his head away and flicks his tail a few times. "I suppose the fantasist would say your dream represents a desire to leave your cage."

"Why would he want that?" says Fay, popping into the conversation. "He's got his own world in there."

You look at her to make sure she is floating in water and not in the air. Her fins sway with their usual elegance under invisible ripples of water.

"I hadn't thought of that," you say. "Leaving my cage." You drop to your lower perch and look into reflections of your eyes in the mirror you hate.

Kaz twists on the floor so he faces you. "It's not safe out there. Caged birds live much longer than wild birds."

"Why?" asks Fay.

"Same reason fish in the sea do not live as long as fish in bowls. Predators."

Fay spins in a quick circle. "What are those?"

"There are fish in the sea, giant monsters really, that eat other fish," Kaz says. "Gobble them up in one bite."

"I don't believe that," says Fay as she swims into her tunnel, where she lingers hidden from view.

You look over to Kaz to ask a follow-up question, but the thought leaves your mind as the window draws your attention. Actually, not the window itself, but the figure you see through its unfocused lens.

It's a bird.

You've never seen a bird in the window before.

It scrapes its beak against the glass and chirps, but you can't make out what it is saying.

"That looks like the bird from my dream, well, a blurry version of it!"

Kaz rises and saunters toward the window.

"What is he saying?" you ask.

Kaz jumps to the seat of Man's stool and puts his ear to the glass. His whiskers twitch, much like the time you saw him playing with the ball of yarn. "Can't say," he replies with distance in his voice. He lifts his paw to the glass.

"Don't scare him away!"

The bird doesn't flinch. Its body separated from Kaz's claws by a slim pane of glass, it looks into the cat's paw. Scratches at the glass again with its beak and lets out a blast of tweets.

Though you can't hear the specific contours of the sound through the window, you sense that is the voice of the bird in your dream—the one you couldn't hear.

And then it's off, in flight.

The only bird you've ever seen other than yourself is gone.

8

Viv

"All he seems to puzzle-ize are maps now," you say.

Kaz's face is disapproving. "Puzzle-ize is not a word."

"I like it," Fay pipes in. "Puzzle-ize, puzzle-ize, come in every shape and size," she chants in a singsongy loop.

Kaz motions to Fay, shaking his head. "Now look what you've done."

For weeks, Man has painted and then puzzle-ized maps. Some are mostly green. Others have the squiggliest waterways. A few, according to Kaz, depict the whole Earth. This doesn't make sense, since Kaz says the Earth is a sphere, yet the map is flat—but you don't press the issue.

The particulars of the maps vary—shifting hues for the land formations, some with the wind-blowing angels, some without, creatures of various types on the land and in the water, most with scribbly words—but all are maps.

As the light in the window dwindles, Man removes the clamp and picks up the last piece of his latest map. He rubs a rough-looking paper along its edges and blows the resulting dust off its surface. Wipes it clean with his handkerchief.

After placing the puzzle piece in a shallow wooden box with the other pieces, he slides a lid into a precut groove at the top of the box and carries it out of the room.

You've noticed the air grows colder as the days get shorter. You're relieved when Man walks in with a fresh log.

The fire blazing again and the oil lamp lit, the room is warm and bright.

He hums what you think is intended to be a happy tune, but, like his whistling, the melody leaves much to be desired.

He places a box on the table and takes out the elements of what has become his evening project—the one that began with the thin, twisting pieces of wood.

From these elements, he creates a three-tiered tower that tapers as it rises. Each level has a seven-sided base held in place by ornate pillars—all carved from wood by Man. Each floor of the tower contains a colorful scene of figurines. Most of the finer points are too small for you to make out.

Kaz pops onto the table to inspect.

Man mumbles and moves him a little more than a paw's length away from his project but lets him stay on the table.

"What do you see?" you ask.

"The bottom is a family—a mother and father and baby," Kaz says. "The middle is three men with crooks in their hands and sheep at their feet."

"Crooks?" you say.

"Staffs. Sticks that curve at the top."

"And the top level?"

"Angels."

"Making wind, like in the maps?"

"No . . . well, I suppose, in a sense. They hold instruments, horns of some sort, up to their mouths."

You, Kaz, and Fay watch as Man places red candles into seven wooden cups secured around the base. Then he slots the blades—twelve in all, each with a star etched in its surface—into an inverted cone rising out of the top of the structure.

"What is it?" you ask Kaz.

"I don't know," he says. You can see in his gaze and hear in his tone that he is engrossed in the spectacle.

Man steps aside to the fireplace mantle and pulls a stick from a metal vase.

You all hear sounds emanating from outside of the room—a door opening and closing. The rumble of human voices.

Man's face is bright like the fire that blazes in the hearth. He tosses the stick onto the table next to his project, plops Kaz back down on the floor, and leaves the room.

Sometime later, Man returns, leading a small human by the hand. In his other hand, he carries a paper rolled into a cylinder and wrapped with a red ribbon, itself tied into a looping bow.

You are fascinated by the little human, a female you can tell.

She sparkles and vibrates with energy.

She has tiny dots on her cheeks and her orange hair is pulled into some kind of tails on either side of her head.

You have never seen a human other than Man before. "I didn't know they came in smaller sizes."

"She's a child," Kaz says. "She's still growing."

"Ah, I see. What is that around her neck?"

"It's a necklace with a pendant." Kaz walks closer to her. "Looks like a flower, a lily."

Man's fingers tug the red ribbon with care. He places the ribbon on the table and unrolls the paper.

Holds it up in the light of his oil lamp and lets out a gasp of joy.

You don't quite see why he is so impressed. It's similar to the blue swirl on his wall. Though, you will admit, the swirls are more precise—circles that appear to descend downward. The colors and shading make it look like it's a shape that cuts into the earth.

You are proud of yourself for your increasing ability to interpret the abstractions of Man and now this new person.

"What do you call this small, female version of a human?" you ask Kaz.

"Well, in general, that is a girl. But Man has called her Viv, so that must be her name."

Viv, you think to yourself and feel a flush of warmth spread through your wings.

"And," Kaz continues, "she has called him Pap several times. Apparently, that is his name."

"Pap?" you say. "I don't think I can call him that. I've known him as Man for too long."

"Agreed."

Fay nods her head, causing a bubble to escape her mouth.

Man pins the new picture to the wall next to the initial blue one, which you have now surmised must have been drawn by Viv as well. He gives her a hug and offers what Kaz tells you are words of gratitude for her gift.

Viv turns and stares at the chessboard. Picks up a figure that looks like the head of a horse and begins to move it around in a gallop. As it tips another piece, Man reaches over and returns both to their places.

Man pulls his stool up to the table and sits Viv on top of it. He grabs the stick he had dropped upon her arrival, dips its tip into the fireplace, and uses it as a torch to light the candles on his project.

He extinguishes the flame in the oil lamp.

Man does achieve some splendid stunts. Somehow, the scenes on the three tiers and the twelve blades extending from the cone at its peak now spin without him even touching them.

Shadow projections of the scenes, which amplify larger than you and even Kaz, dance on the walls of the room. But what attracts your attention is Viv's face, aglow in candlelight, in wonder as she watches her gift twirl in a peaceful revolution as if it is magic. Maybe it is.

∞

You fall asleep and wake up thinking about Viv— her freshness, her spark. Qualities you have sensed in yourself but never expressed that you can remember. Perhaps when you were new to the world?

And to your delight, not long after light fills the window, she enters the room.

This time, she zips straight to your cage. Her eyes are wide open as are yours, two intrigued beings.

She stands on her tippy toes, lifts her arm, and puts her finger between two poles toward the bottom of your cage. You hop down to the cage floor and press the smooth curve of your beak against her finger.

You tingle in the connection.

Man, who walked in behind her, pulls her hand back. He speaks to her, presumably telling her not to put her finger in your cage, though Kaz is not here to decipher his words for you.

Viv's exiting hand leaves your cage gently swaying at the end of the brass chain that attaches to the ceiling.

You would bite Man if you could for interrupting your exchange with Viv.

She smiles at you but then moves on to Fay's bowl. You're not bragging, but Viv does not look as excited upon viewing Fay. Fish aren't as captivating as birds, so that makes sense.

She heads back toward you, but Man intercepts her. Plucks her right up off the ground and places her on his stool. He scoots the girl and the stool to the edge of the table and lays out one of his puzzles for her.

Viv lets out a vocal communication that sounds exhilarating.

You're surprised that the puzzle is not of a map. In fact, as her little fingers explore the pieces and bring them into some semblance of order, you realize it is the puzzle that Man made of you.

You hop from upper to lower and back to your upper perch as you watch her make progress.

Man offers some guidance, helping her place the corners and edges of the puzzle together, forming a frame.

Viv takes it from there as Man picks up his hurdy-gurdy and plays a fanciful accompaniment to her restoration of your image.

After some time, there, in completion, is a picture of you.

You couldn't be more proud when she giggles in glee, looking at you, at the puzzle, then back at you.

You do not hop between perches anymore. You stand tall and puff out your chest.

Unfortunately, in moments of triumph, disaster lurks.

Viv's face drops. Is it a look of concentration? Disappointment?

You trace the line of her vision to your chest. Looking down, you see the bare spot of exposed skin in an otherwise fluffy array of plumage.

You had forgotten about your habit of plucking feathers. Since Viv's arrival, it had not entered your mind or actions once. But when you rose to your full stature, the perverse monument of its past occurrences became more pronounced. Your habit, it turns out, had not forgotten about you.

A shame you have never felt before burns in you—from the top of your head to the tips of your wings.

You shrink. This contracts the featherless, scabby section of your chest, making it less prominent. But your spirit shrinks, too.

Man directs Viv's attention back to the puzzle. Booms of sound followed by his lips spreading wide into a smile. He points at the puzzle, then to her art on the wall.

And when she looks away, you thrust your beak into your chest and deplume a small region—feather after feather after feather.

9

Illusion

The feather's shaft is lifeless in your beak. Dead cells, like the dead cell in which you perch.

You raise your head in slow motion this time.

Feel the quill glide along and out of its sheath, the follicle that moments before clung to the feather for dear life.

There is an attendant sensation. You cannot tell if it is pleasure or pain. Though when the sensation ceases, there is a feeling of relief. Like the relief that comes when you wonder if something bad might happen and then the bad thing happens—it is the relief of no longer being tempted by hope.

The relief is fleeting.

The sole way to restore the relief is to go back in. Take hold of a plume—useless on your chest, in your cage, in your world—and draw it out.

Spread your mandibles and reject the meaning of the feather. The path it cuts through the air in its clumsy fall reminds you of the meandering notes of Man's whistle.

∽

Viv is placed at Man's table. Another morning, another puzzle.

This one is of Kaz.

Viv is focused on pressing together two pieces that do not fit.

You keep your back to her so she can't see your chest should she look up. But you track her every expression, her every movement, in quick glances over your shoulder.

Man is in and out.

At one point he exits and another human, a full-size female, peeks her head in. This person is younger than Man but much older than Viv. Long, yellowy-white hair is wrapped up around her head in an elaborate pattern. Kaz tells you it is the girl's mother.

She enters, kisses Viv on the top of her head, and then stares at the chessboard, one hand cupping her chin.

Man returns.

Viv's mother moves a light chess piece so that it takes the place of one of Man's dark pieces. She places the captured figurine on the side of the board, folds her arms, and looks quite pleased with herself.

Man puts his hand on the visitor's shoulder, and the two leave the room.

Kaz's tail traces a semi-circle around his hindquarters; one eye is below his feet and the other is way too high to be part of a natural-looking face—at least the puzzle version of Kaz looks that way.

The real Kaz is on the far side of the room in a corner you've never seen him occupy before. "This little beast has an insatiable penchant for grabbing my tail. Ghastly manners."

His critique elicits a giggle and a couple of bubbles from Fay.

"I wouldn't laugh too hard," Kaz says, his tail tucked out of sight. "If she isn't afraid to get her hands wet, I'm sure you'll find yourself missing a fin or two."

Fay scrunches her face and shakes it side-to-side. "Not that sweet creature."

The sounds of the words pass you by, bounce off the wall behind you, and obliterate into nonexistence.

Viv leaves puzzle-Kaz in disarray.

She's off the stool.

Fay ducks into her tunnel, not so confident of the girl's sweetness now that she is in arm's reach of her bowl.

But Viv doesn't notice as she passes by and makes her way to Man's desk. She collects paper, scissors, string, pen, and inkwell. Off to a shelf. On her toes, stretching her arm to its limit . . . she clutches two jars of paint and a brush.

Back to the table. She lays out her loot.

Cobbled together from your intermittent glimpses, her activity unfolds as a sequence of disjointed motions, though you can hear that each item is actually arranged on the table with care.

You steal another look. Caught. She is looking at you.

You look down and see the mirror, which you realize can be a barrier. A quick hop and twist, and you can sneak more peeks. The downside is you must see your reflection between each peek. Unintentional viewing of a grim bird for a glimpse of this child in the act of creation. A fair trade.

Scissors cut rough circles out of white paper. You see her tongue slip out the side of her mouth as if it provides balance to her hand as she works.

Little fingers grip the pen, dip its tip into the inkwell, and then scratch the outline of a bird onto one of the circles.

On the other circle, they draw an orby cage.

Viv is much faster with the paint than Man, though a bit less refined, too. The bird now has color, similar to your own, smudged onto mostly the right places. The black ink of the cage is widened with a thick stroke of brown.

She hops off the stool.

Fay, who had swum to the surface of the water for a bite of food, dashes back into her tunnel empty-mouthed.

Viv now stands before the hearth, waving the two miniature paintings back and forth in the warm air of the fire. You watch the liquid glimmer of the paint disappear into dryness.

Back at the table, child hands bind the pictures, back-to-back, by weaving string through pairs of holes on either end of the circles.

Without moving her head, she lifts her eyes to you.

You do not look away, though you keep your chest obscured by the mirror.

She places her art in the front pocket of her dress. Drags the stool across the bumps in the wooden floorboards and places it before you. She climbs its one step and finds a precarious balance standing upon its seat.

Viv retrieves the project from her pocket. Pinches the ends of the pair of strings between her fingers and twists them over and over and over again. They begin to curl up into knotty clumps.

She lifts her arms so her painted bird faces you, so close you could reach out with your beak and peck it.

"Looks like she made you a leash," Kaz meows from his corner of the room. "It's been nice knowing you."

You do not budge.

Viv pulls the tips of the strings and the wheel flips end-over-end between her hands. You see a bird . . . a cage . . . a bird . . . a cage. As the frequency of their tumbling climaxes, the two pictures merge into one, and you view the single image of a condemned prisoner—a caged bird.

You lower your head, clench a mouthful of feathers in your beak, and tear.

Without intervention, you don't know if Viv would have ever stopped twisting that image before you. Rubbing it in your face, another mirror revealing your captivity; your life, your existence—watching others live. Knowing you have no choice!

Man walks in and scolds her, for standing on the stool, according to Kaz. No mention of her torment of you, but at least this puts an end to her taunt.

Back on the floor, she zigzags through the room, arms out, flapping, though the motion produces no lift. Singing out a silly melody of high-pitched *la, la, las.* More mockery of you?

Man sets her back at the table and begins to return his stolen objects to their places on his desk and shelf. He spills some ink from the well on his shirt—something for which you have seen him slam his fist down on the table in anger in the past. But this time, he dabs at the spot with his thumb and laughs—even though it is her fault.

He picks up Viv's cruel wheel. You fear he will twist it as she did, but instead, he drops it into his drawer with a smile.

Why is he smiling? Does he not understand? What spell does this little ghoul have on him?

You hop to your upper perch, your pitiful chest on display, and you look upon both humans with contempt.

Viv lifts her finger but not in your direction. She points at Fay's fishbowl. And there, on top of the water, floats Fay. She is not floating above the water as in your dream. She is not retrieving a bite of food.

You cry out.

She does not speak or even release a bubble in reply. Her fins are still. Eyes blank.

You don't understand.

Man pulls a rag out of his pocket and places it over the bowl so Fay is no longer visible. He returns to the table and guides the hands of the girl as she puts Kaz's eyes into place in the puzzle.

Man mumbles in what sounds like a sad tone as they complete the puzzle.

"Now she can't see!" you yell to Kaz. "Fay likes to look around the room from her bowl, but that rag blocks her view."

Kaz looks to the bowl, then to you. He lowers his head.

Man takes Viv by the hand and walks her to the door.

She breaks free and runs to the space below your cage. She speaks in a soft voice, waving her hand. You assume she is belittling you—that you, a bird, do not have hands like she does, or some such cruelty.

You look away.

Man and the girl leave the room.

Viv entered your life on a wave of hope. She exits your judge. You hate her.

10

Bumblebird

You hear a door beyond the room close, and the manor takes on a familiar stillness only disrupted by the occasional shuffling about of Man.

He walks into the room. Removes the rag from Fay's bowl. With his finger and thumb, he picks up what Kaz has explained is Fay's corpse by the tail fin. Places her in the palm of his other hand, and, with Kaz at his side, leaves the room.

It makes no sense to you. To be alive, with no memory of beginning, and then to cease as Kaz describes it?

You do not understand death. But you feel it in Fay's absence.

You think Man and Kaz understand it less than you do.

Not even a week passes before Man walks in with a jar in his hand, Kaz his shadow.

What you see inside causes you to bounce between perches without willing the physical exultation. It's Fay! Thrashing in wild jolts in a jar with barely enough space to spin around.

Wait.

"What is that gold stripe down her back? That wasn't there before," you say.

Kaz's tail flits in loose coordination with the fish's movements in the jar. "That's not Fay. Well, Man named this one Fay as well. But it's not the Fay that used to be here. As I told you, Man dug a small hole outside, dropped Fay—the former Fay—in it, and filled it with dirt."

Kaz's eyes open wide as Man dumps this replacement Fay, Faux Fay, you call her, in the bowl straight from the jar. She begins to swim and explore—as if it is her bowl. In Fay's water. Amidst her plants. Through her tunnel.

Your heart sinks.

∞

Blue phantoms whip up into yellow and orange and hot white wisps, pyramids of fire. The hearth has never blazed so bright. You can feel the heat on your face. Pleasant at first, but then too much. You scoot backward on your perch. Your cage shifts toward the flames as if the whole room is tipping forward.

There is no way your cage could reach the fireplace. You've looked at the brass chain connecting it to the ceiling countless times, and it's not long enough. Yet your cage creeps closer and closer as the heat intensifies. You look up, and the chain elongates, like the taffy you've watched Man eat before, in long gooey strands.

You try to cry out, but your lung-emptying screech carries no sound.

Another dream?

It must be, but the terror is real.

You notice the fire, too, is silent, with no crackle to accompany its fury.

You search the room.

Kaz sits on Man's stool in front of the easel and paints a picture of Viv—complete with dots on her cheeks and the lily dangling from her neck. Her visage sneers at you.

You watch the painting separate into puzzle pieces on its own, without the touch of a blade.

The fishbowl is surrounded by fire, Faux Fay tossing about in the water by bubbles rising from the sand below.

You look to the lower perch, and there is the bird. He's on the side of the cage closest to the fire, scraping at the latch.

You hop down to the lower perch but are pushed to the back of the cage by the fierce heat.

The bird turns to face you, his wings outstretched, alight in flames.

∽

You awaken gasping for air, though the room, of course, has no smoke and no fire.

Kaz is nowhere to be seen, as he had left the room earlier in the evening with Man. Faux Fay is still asleep in her non-bubbling bowl of water.

You look to the window, and there he is on the ledge again. The bird of your dream?

He scrapes at the window with his beak, and unlike the bird of your dream, you can hear him chirping. As in the time before, the sound is too muted by the glass to quite make out what he is saying.

You try to interpret the bird—the dream, the scraping, his presence outside—as you did Viv's wheel, as a confirmation of your doom. But you cannot complete the dark thought, which winds into your mind in a twisting knot and comes back out a radiating beam of light.

You look to your chest, but you have no urge to deplume; there is nothing you feel that needs to be relieved.

And the thought takes shape as vivid as the bird's fiery wings in your dream: You will leave your cage—today.

∞

Kaz curls up in front of the morning fire as paint, by Man's command, squiggles into land and water on the easel.

The warmth of that first fire each day always feels good to you. Though, lately you reject its comfort, reminding yourself that a temperate cage is still a cage.

But not today.

The bird might have left the window ledge as Kaz and Man arrived in the room, but the hope he sparked continues to surge within you. The pleasure of the hearth remains. The colors Man applies to his painting glisten in a silvery light that washes through your mind in an easy stream. The sound of Kaz's purr, inspiration for a song.

Kaz glances in your direction. "What's gotten into you?"

You assume the lilt in your song reached his ears.

You don't say a word to Kaz about your dream, the bird, or your plan—well, not really a plan but a reality you will manifest. You have wondered whether you should trust the cat after his nonchalant response to Fay's death and replacement. You have a strong feeling that he would react the same way should you die.

"Oh, just the freshness of a new day."

You look over to Faux Fay.

It occurs to you that it is not the fault of this new fish that she was dumped into Fay's bowl and even given Fay's name. No, thinking of her as Faux Fay is not fair.

"Wouldn't you agree, Fay, that it's a beautiful day?" you say.

Fay looks confused. Probably because she has tried to communicate with you several times since her arrival, and you acted as if she didn't exist.

You look into her eyes, and a bubble escapes her open mouth.

You decide now would be a great time to make amends with her. "I'm sorry, Fay, that I ignored you before. I sorely miss the prior occupant of your bowl, but that is no excuse for my rude behavior. Welcome."

"Oh. Well, thank you."

And so goes the morning. Man paints while Kaz purrs and Fay swims. And you are a bird who will leave your cage today.

∞

Man enters the room with a cup of water in the crook of his arm and his hand in a light fist, surely holding seeds. That water and food are for you. That means he will be opening your cage door. That means it is time.

You've always seen the door to your cage as an entry point from the outside world—for man's hand. Today, for the first time, you see it as an exit.

Man opens the door.

You fly out.

You wobble about the air in a way that reminds you of one time when Kaz ran into the room too hastily and couldn't catch his footing on the wood floor. Limbs shot out in all directions with little success in taming his trajectory.

And now your limbs shoot out in all directions. Legs flailing without the stability provided by your perch, wings in a chaotic flutter, and your head bobbling around with no real focus.

You discover that life in a cage produces a vexing circumstance: You have a hard time leaving a space in the air that is larger than your cage. You desire to fly straight to the door that leads out of the room. Instead, you cut back each time you reach a distance that approximates the diameter of the cage, as if you have encountered some invisible barrier. You make only the tiniest progress forward with each circle.

In addition to that, jumping from perch to perch is not the same as flying in even the limited space of the room. Your wings keep you afloat, but their thrust lacks force and harmony.

And then there is Man.

He is about as graceful as you in the melee.

First to go is the water. The wooden cup crashes into the floor, spraying its contents all around.

Next are the seeds from his hand, the smallest bit landing in your cage as intended. The rest scatter as he tries to grab you.

You are successful in escaping his grasp as his fingers close on the palm of his hand without you inside. But your slow advance toward the door as you bumble in cage-sized ellipses is no match for Man's swiftness.

After you elude several of his swipes, he lunges for the door and slams it shut.

The window does not open. The fireplace is ablaze. The room is now your cage, for there is no way to escape. Since you can't fly out, you fly up.

11

Relativity

Your eyes follow the curving line as it spirals, smaller and smaller and smaller, to a point. You hop to the right and do the same with the next spiral.

You've studied the patterns at the space where the wall meets the ceiling many times before, though always from your cage. Perched on its ledge, you are amazed by the sophistication of the design now that you are seeing it up close. Each spiral is bigger than you. The flowers filling the spaces between these swirls are carved with a delicate touch—curled stems, fanning leaves, and soft petals projecting from the wall in relief. Dead wood, all of it, yet impressive in its details. You wonder if it's the product of Man's hands.

Kaz stands below you. "What has gotten into you?"

"I don't want to live in a cage anymore."

"Well, Man is not going to allow you to live outside of the cage in this room."

"The room is not where I want to be."

Kaz motions to the window with his head. "I've told you, it's not safe out there."

You look down to Man.

He nudges Kaz out of his way with a leg of the stool and sets it down. You sense anger in the abruptness of his actions and the tones of his words.

"It doesn't seem that safe in here," you say.

"Oh, he won't hurt you."

Man climbs on the stool and slowly lifts his hand toward you.

"He takes care of you," Kaz adds.

You've proven to yourself that you cannot fly far in a straight line, so you flit out in a tight semi-circle, then another, away from Man.

Yes, that is definitely anger you hear in his voice as he climbs down from the stool to move it below your new location.

You realize that this ledge upon which you stand stretches around the perimeter of the room, like one long, four-sided perch. Given the amount of time it takes for Man to relocate his stool, you figure you can dodge him all day long.

The objects of the room you have always viewed from your cage look surreal, even disorienting, from your new perspective. It's like one of Man's puzzles before the pieces have been assembled.

The ledge is huge. Most of the rest of the objects are smaller than they look from your cage. The relativity of size makes everything appear impermanent, less inevitable than before. The desk, chair, table, bookshelf, easel, and paint—all props with ephemeral meanings. Man's stool becomes a ladder to extend his body toward you. And as you shift to a new space, your action transforms the ladder into a pedestal displaying a frustrated Man.

Fay's bowl looks like a tiny cup of water and Kaz like the kitten he was when you met him, a fraction of his usual size.

You've never challenged Kaz before, but his diminished stature and your lofty perch make you bold. "You say it's dangerous out there, but you're out there . . . sometimes."

Kaz focuses on the position of his tail in relation to the legs of the pedestal, which becomes a ladder again as Man scoots it toward your new location. "And that's how I know it's dangerous."

You dart out from the wall and land, this time, on top of the bookshelf. Under your feet, the bookshelf becomes a tree, or more of a monument to the tree it once was.

And from there you see it.

Your cage.

Or is it *your* cage? You are choosing for it not to be now, having exchanged its barriers for the barriers of the room.

Like the stool that became a ladder and then a pedestal, you see the impermanence of the cage. It was a concave snare; now it's a small ball. If it fell to the ground, Kaz would likely bat it around like he did the yarn. If in the sky, perhaps it would chase the moon.

But *your* cage? Says who?

"Says Man."

"I suppose I was thinking . . . speaking out loud," you say.

"Yes," Kaz replies.

Man stands, mumbling something, with his hands on his hips.

Kaz flicks his tail side-to-side now that the immobile stool leg is no longer a threat, at least for the time being. "Food, water, warmth. That is life in your cage."

"Food, water, warmth, and nothing else. And those things do not exist out there?" you say, motioning toward the window.

"The food you must secure for yourself. The same with the water. And when you search for them, there are predators that will be searching for you. The warmth comes and goes. The sun brings heat, often more than you want; then the night takes it away and leaves in its place a breathtaking chill this time of year. And I assure you, there is no hearth."

"But compared to this cage, there is so much space. You have said so yourself."

"Yes. So much space that you will be lost. You have no idea."

"I saw it on my way in here," says Fay.

You look down at her through the surface of her water as she whips a brisk loop through the rock tunnel. "And what did you see?"

"It's like a bowl that has no end. Looked rather dry though. And the light! The sun was so bright, I had to close my eyes after a few moments."

The conversation lulls you into a world of thoughts that are not your own. You see Man moving, but you've seen him move so many times before that you forget he is coming for you. This time he turns his chair into a ladder and raises his hand to you. Just his finger, as if he wants you to turn it into your perch.

Without thinking it through, you lash out, bite his finger as hard as you can, and fly off in your ellipses as confused in your thoughts as you are in your flight pattern.

Man pops his finger in his mouth as you detect an odd metallic taste in your own. You touch down atop the panel of wood resting on the easel. Another map. This one round.

Now Man lunges for you.

In your haste, you release waste, adding what looks like a streak of white paint on an otherwise green section of the map. You swirl upward as you approach Viv's downward spiraling drawings on the wall.

Man is closing in, but you hover in front of the child's artwork for a moment. Seeing the pictures up close makes you think of her and fills you with fury. You grab one in your beak and tear it, then claw the other, in passing, as you race to a new section of the ledge near the ceiling.

You hear Man make a noise you've never heard before. It is accompanied by his face changing colors, something else you've never experienced. Kaz has told you about lizards that change colors to match their environment, but Man's new scarlet hue does the opposite.

He pushes the chair aside and returns to the stool, turning it again into a ladder. But before he gets anywhere near you, the stool changes itself into a slide that leads to a swift trip into the floor for Man.

His crash landing shakes the room.

Man discharges a sound that reminds you of the shriek Kaz made that time he fell asleep with his tail a little too close to the fireplace.

And then it is calm.

Kaz squeezes his body into the far corner of the room.

Fay freezes in her tunnel.

You sit on your ledge.

And Man gets up from the floor. His movements are labored. His hand presses into his lower back as his face scrunches and becomes small.

He looks at you, then at the door.

He picks up one of his larger paintbrushes and waves it at you.

You circle away from the brush and alight on a spot on the ledge near the hearth.

Man opens the door, steps outside, though his eyes are fixed on you, and closes it behind him.

You feel a gust of air leave the room with him as a breath is pulled from your lungs.

12

Stand Your Ground

You realize from your ledge perch that an urge, in this case to live outside of your cage, does not constitute a plan. The urge got you out of your spherical cage but into another, that of the cubical room.

You decide that you will cease being mesmerized by your new perspective of the room and instead create a strategy that will lead you to the space that transcends geometrical enclosures.

You've seen Man leave the room so many times. Your view through the open door reveals not what you picture to be the outside world, but another room of some sort.

Kaz lies on his side, his forepaw angled upward, licking the pad of his foot.

You flit down in clumsy loops to the windowsill. "How do I get out there? It looks like there's another room outside of this door."

He stops cleaning himself. "It's futile."

You take a brief look through the window, which up close allows you to see a larger area than before, though it is, as always, obscured by the frosted glass. You have a fleeting hope that the bird of your dream, the bird who has appeared on the other side of this pane, will be there, but there is no time for that now. Man could return any moment.

You hop down to a leg of the overturned stool, which your arrival turns into a perch. "It's futile to think I can truly live within those bars or even in this room."

Kaz rises.

He reaches forward with his front paws as far as they stretch, the muscles in his back and arms rippling beneath his fur. You watch his claws protract, slinking through their sheaths, and dig into the floorboards. You hear them scratching the wood as he draws them back into his paws.

He stands to his full height and moves toward you.

You have never been this close to him before.

You watch the bones under the skin of his shoulders pivot up and down; the motion is graceful but also unnerving.

He increases in size with each step he takes. You remember him saying he is much larger in his dreams. You wonder if you are in one of his dreams right now, as he is gigantic and growing.

You watched the stool become a ladder and then a pedestal. Does Kaz look at you, outside of your cage, and see a ball of yarn? Or worse yet, a meal? You do not know, but there is a wild sparkle in his eye.

You cut an arcing semi-circle in the air back up to the windowsill.

Kaz continues his approach.

You want to expand your distance from Kaz, but you need him. He knows how to get outside. Flying away might offend him or cause him to lose interest. You decide to stand your ground.

He lifts his paws and places them inches from your feet. Raises his head, which is now two or three times your size, until he is eye-to-eye with you.

You note the subtle flaring and contracting of his nostrils. Waves of his breath break over you, a moist, warm air with a fleshy scent.

You wish there would be a purr in his throat, a sign that he is in a good mood, but there is not.

"Outside of this room," the giant feline says, "is a hallway."

"Oh. And that leads outside?"

"The hallway opens up into other rooms. Most with windows like the one behind you, which I have never seen open; I do not believe they can open. There's a stairway behind one door that leads up to a rooftop patio. Another to the bottom floor of the manor, where there are more hallways and rooms. There is one enormous room with a door that leads outside. Like the door to the roof, there is no way to know when Man will open it. As I said, it is futile to try to leave."

"Well, can you describe how to get to these doors?"

"They are intricate paths filled with obstacles, at least on the ground. These took me many days to learn to navigate. But I imagine you would be flying in the air. I wouldn't know that path."

"Maybe you can guide me?" Your voice quivers as you notice that, this close, each of Kaz's eyes is larger than your head.

His ears flatten backward as he opens his mouth wide. White, sharp teeth. Tongue curling down and toward you. Whiskers projecting in an outline of your body.

You feel your muscles tighten, unable to move; you are paralyzed by the smell of death on his breath.

You consider, in horror, that your imprecise request might be answered by the beast removing you from the manor by way of you traveling in his gut.

You have never been so relieved to see that Kaz is yawning.

He closes his mouth and returns his forepaws to the floor. "This bores me," he says as he ambles back to his spot in front of the hearth.

Your eyes leave Kaz, pause on the cage, and then fix themselves on the door.

∞

It's hard to believe that leaving the room requires so much waiting.

You don't know how long you've been perched above the door on the wall's ledge, but you find yourself pacing back and forth to keep your blood flowing.

Your moment arrives. You even have a forewarning as you hear Man's heavy steps approach.

You are disappointed to realize that your plan is no more than to fly through the door when it opens; then stay high on the wall until you work your way to the next door based on Kaz's vague description. Not much of an improvement on the plan-free urge that propelled you out of your cage in the first place.

You look down and see the doorknob twist.

A dark space between the door and the wall appears and then widens.

Man's eyes look upward, searching for you, you presume. But they do not see you as they scan a section of ledge across the room.

You set all your focus on flying straight—straight into the center of the darkness that is neither door nor wall.

You launch.

Instead of straight, you curve into a cage-shaped circle that takes you away from the portal before bending you back in its direction.

That diversion, and the accompanying mad flapping of your wings, allows Man to advance into the room and shove the door back toward the wall.

Time pours out in a slow ooze . . . You feel the massive slab of wood press into your tail feathers, forcing you toward the doorframe on a path that will result in a crushed skull and torso if you proceed. Instinct drives you up and away from the door. As you push your wings downward, the door compresses the feathers and flesh and bones of your right wing into the tiny space between itself and the frame. The sound of the slamming door and your crunching wing reach your ears in a punishing harmony.

The door is now a trap.
Relentless time resumes its pace.

13

Bird in the Hand

You now know what it is like to flap your left wing with all your might, while your right wing is trapped between a door and its frame, with the goal of not having that wing rip out of its socket. It is the collision of sizzling pain and icy panic.

You are a series of frantic reactions to circumstance, despite it being a circumstance you helped incite.

The harder you flap, the greater the pain, but you fear stopping will be worse.

You look over your shoulder and see the cage. It hangs in stasis—no pleasure, but no pain. Was it so bad?

Your mind dives into the joint connecting your left wing to your body. Bones, muscles, ligaments, tendons rise and fall with a popping twist at the crests and troughs of an erratic wave.

Feathers grasp at air.

Lungs gasp for the same.

The gas flees faster than it is replaced.

It would help if you could stop screaming, but you are not willing the sounds, so you have no command over them.

You feel your heart beat below a featherless section of your chest. The pounding is so rapid you experience it as a single swelling of the muscle rather than a succession of pulses.

Another glimpse of the cage. Your cage. A place where, not long ago, your wing was not being crushed.

You feel your stomach expel its contents; you choke on regret.

At that moment, the trap becomes a door—an open door.

An act of mercy? Is Man letting you go? Or is he releasing the door's grip on you just to slam it again, this time on your head to take your life?

Your wing now free, you feel yourself fall as you see Man's hand reach out.

Your right wing, to your surprise, begins to move, though not in coordination with your left.

Out of the room would be ideal, straight up would suffice, but the circle is your path. The habitual arc you trace draws you toward Man's head. You have seen his face up close many times before when he brings food and water to your cage, but never this close. It is now immense and dynamic, a shifting combination of concern, confusion, and even fear.

You hear the door close.

Your loopy trajectory sweeps you up the plane of his forehead. You feel a tail feather graze his skin.

He jerks his head backward as he thrusts his hand toward you.

You dash up, just out of the range of his greedy fingers, but then circle back toward them again. Several more of these flailing passes, each missing Man's flailing hands, lift you up toward the ledge near the ceiling, this time to the area over the window.

You see the air stir as you flap your wings to stabilize your landing—a whirlwind of dust with detached feathers, down and flight, jostling about its funnel. A fine mist of blood sprays into the space around you, onto the carvings of swirls and flowers in the dead wood, and into your eyes.

Fire crackles. Fay swims. Man paints.

The dust settled hours ago.

The new cage of the room, you discover, feels worse than the old one, which still hangs, door open, from its brass chain. The new cage is dominated by a quality you never knew before your attempted escape—uncertainty.

Man has hardly glanced your way since you landed above the window. At least when he looked your way and tried to catch you earlier, you had a pretty good guess as to what he was thinking. You have not a clue now.

He has left the room a few times. On each occasion, he closed the door behind him and did the same upon his return. The thought arose upon these openings that it had been your desire to leave the room, but your body offered no response.

You're not even sure you can fly. You no longer bleed, but your injured wing stiffens beneath a sticky scab, a steely bolt of pain accompanying each throb of your heart.

You look down to Kaz. Perhaps he has some insight. Some . . . anything, anything other than the chaotic thoughts in your head.

He shakes his head at you with a smug look on his face.

You keep your mouth closed and avert your eyes as your head sinks.

You know where you are, but you are indeed lost.

∞

You have no memory of pain like this.

Nor do you have memories of extreme hunger or thirst, yet you experience both now. At the slightest urge for food or water, for as long as you can remember, you were no more than a hop away from satiation. Not so now. This makes you think of Kaz's warnings of life on the outside, where such things must be sought out.

But where are they in here?

There is no food to be seen. Not even a roll of bread as Man sometimes has on the table before him.

And the water?

He does not have a cup with him.

Fay's bowl?

"Don't even think about it," says Fay.

"Thinking . . . speaking out loud again?" you say.

"Yes," the fish replies. "And you know exactly where there's water for you." She wiggles her snout in the direction of your old cage. "That is your world."

You wonder why there is so little difference between the new Fay and the old Fay. They are two separate beings but seemingly of one mind.

∞

You don't truly understand time, but you watch as the light brightens and then slips away from the window below you.

On Man's latest entry into the room, he walks to your cage, places a handful of food in your dish, and fills your water from a cup. He breaks off a piece of bread, topped with those little seeds you like, and places it on top of the other food in your cage.

The food would be nice. You hunger in a way you never have before, but you cannot keep your eyes off the water. You realize that in the excited lead-up to your escape, you had not taken a sip of water all day—and you can't remember when you last drank yesterday. Your thirst increases to the point of torment.

The room is now lit by Man's oil lamp. The mysterious moon is nowhere in sight beyond the window, which is now black. When Man leaves for the night, you will be on this ledge in the dark.

He opens a letter at his desk, then sits on the stool and stairs at the chessboard. Moves a light piece one square forward and slides a dark piece several spots diagonally. Back to his desk. He sits in the chair and jots something down on a piece of paper.

You only see his movements in your peripheral field as your eyes remain locked on the water in the cage.

You try to swallow, but your mouth is so dry that you just draw air through your beak; the skin in your throat rubs against itself in a scratchy friction.

You didn't see Man pick up the instrument, but the drone of the hurdy-gurdy now fills the room. A long, serpentine howl.

You've never heard him hold a single note that long. It slithers from the machine and melts into you.

Another drone joins the first. This pitch is higher. It wavers above the original like rippling light you have observed over the fireplace.

And then another.

You sense the imminence of the next sounds before he unleashes them—a cascade of barbed notes stabbing the air in an unrelenting riff.

Tones pass through your feathers, overcome your muscles, and penetrate your bones.

They lift your wings and drive them in the pattern that pulls you through space, each flap of your right wing a burning lash of pain.

You cross the room in horizontal loops that edge toward the open door of the cage.

The surface of the water shimmers in the oil lamp's light.

The last convulsion of your will, your desire for freedom, pushes you up so you avoid entering. You land on the outside of the cage and perch on a curved pole directly over the water.

You look down.

Man's hand closes around your body.

∞

You dream.

No sound.

The bird scrapes the latch.

He looks at you, his beak scratched and chipped more severely than before. Blood on his face where a bar has pressed into and cut his flesh.

Back to the latch.

The cage door swings open.

The bird falls out and lands on the ground, inert.

Man picks him up, the bird's body limp—head, tail, and wings dangling toward the floor—and walks out of the room.

14

Meow

It has been several days since the door closed on your wing.

You gag on a sip of water. You were so desperate for it before, but its taste from within the cage is now bitter.

The food has no flavor at all.

You look around the room—the cage that contains your cage. The swirls and flowers carved into the wood ledge, tiny again with distance. Man's apparatus—desk and chair and table and bookshelf and chessboard and stool and easel and paint—no longer dynamic objects to explore but stale artifacts to observe from captivity.

Then there's the door, the slab that crushed your wing. Your nerves flash in dread every time it pops open or creaks to a close.

All is doused in a faint coat of blue. Even the fire. Kaz exists within the same filter, his fur now a whisper of azure. The gold stripe on Fay's back has lost its luster, washing out into a flaccid green.

And there stands Man. Painting a representation of the world outside with the same hand that placed you back in your cage and fastened the latch.

You close your eyes to escape the material reminders of your failure. But the immaterial parade marching through your mind recounts the same story: a Man who would crush you before he would let you be free; a cat who was right; a bird who needed to fly straight, instead flying in irresistible loops.

The immaterial casts a larger shadow than the material, so you open your eyes. And you look into the mirror you hate at the bird you despise.

Your right wing is no longer in symmetry with your left wing. The shocking pain of its initial injury has settled into a continuous background ache that throbs with each inhalation of breath and spikes in intensity every time you move it.

Shift your attention to your face and then to a single eye. You look beyond the convex image of yourself on its glossy exterior. Stare into an empty vault, a shell with no inhabitant. Shapeless. No color, no light. You sense yourself sinking into an expanse that has no bottom.

And there you remain. For hours? For days? It makes no difference.

You listen to the rumblings of Man. The sound of paint squishing off the brush and onto the wood of his latest work. The occasional bubble bursting at the surface of Fay's bowl.

You hear Kaz winding up into activity.

There is impatience in his voice as it throttles between *purrs* and *meows*. You've heard him make these sounds with these inflections thousands of times before, always accompanied by him weaving between Man's legs and then pacing before the door. But in your mirror-induced trance, your mind rushes ahead of reality and envisions the events you know will ensue: Man putting his brush between his teeth and using his now-free hand to open the door; the pattering pads of Kaz's feet growing quieter as they take the cat farther beyond the room; Man closing the door.

You look away from your reflection and watch the real scene unfold, identical to your precognition.

Back in the mirror, back into the void.

Why do you have to be a bird?

If you were a cat, you would simply make some noises and pace about, and you would have the door to the world opened for you. You would be free. You would have the food and water of Man's house and the hearth—but you could leave at will and enjoy the outside world as well.

Are you a bird?

Why not a cat?

What makes you a bird and Kaz a cat?

You watched the stool become a ladder and a slide and a perch depending on how it was used.

You stare into the mirror.

A portal to a new you.

∞

Falling deep into your eye, you sense the barbs of your feathers collapse, spiraling in on themselves, softening into hair; your beak receding into your face, a pink triangle manifesting in its place, framed by twitching whiskers; your fanning tail curling into a furry serpent; wings rolling into meaty cylinders with paws tipped in feline claws with which you will draw the world to yourself.

With your transformation arises an odd sound in your head. Whispers, dissonant where their edges overlap. They're loud, but with focus you turn them down. There—much better.

You invent a trick: As you draw back from the depth of your eye, you keep a part of your mind, as much of it as you can, in that void, maintaining the oblivion of the bird.

You now see your whole face. Gone are your beady eyes. In their place, green pools with a sliver of a raft floating in the middle of each iris, expanding and contracting as if they're alive.

The vision takes your breath away.

You look into the room. To Fay, the fish who will always be a fish. To Kaz, beautiful, perfect Kaz, who has returned to warm himself by the fire. To Man, who creates his own world with a paintbrush. And to the window, dark, the thinnest barrier separating you from the outside.

The whispers remain. Focus.

You open your mouth, and with your loudest voice you make a sound you have never made before.

"Meow."

15

Lights Out

You are a cat in a cage.

You purr and meow.

You're impressed with the accuracy of your sounds and with the volume you are able to project, especially with your meow. You're louder than Kaz. Much louder, and your meow has a more cutting, trebly timbre. It's striking really, maybe even an improvement on the cat's call.

The purr tickles your throat in the most amusing way.

As a bonus, your vocalizations drown out the whispers that otherwise cycle in and out of prominence in your mind.

You can't believe you are still in your cage. Surely Man hears you and will respond as he does to Kaz soon. Then you realize you are not pacing. Pacing is a key element of Kaz's communication.

You move your feet . . . uh, paws . . . on the perch so that you shift back and forth across its length at a speedy clip. Wait! The perch? Cats don't cling to perches.

You hop down to the floor of the cage, the disk-shaped tray that intersects the bottom section of the sphere.

You sense your waste beneath your . . . paws. Not ideal, but until you are out of the cage, it will have to do.

Meowing. Purring. Pacing.

It won't be long now.

You look at your audience. Fay is so fixated on you, she starts to tip sideways. Man turned and stared at you from your first meow. He takes a step closer now and laughs so hard, tears drip from his eyes. Tears of joy at your transformation? Tears of regret for having imprisoned you for so long, and now for keeping a cat in an orbicular cage suspended above the ground?

You doubt both theories, particularly the latter, as Man does not let you out, but returns to his work, exhaling a chuckle every now and then in response to your communications.

Kaz is the first to speak. "What is wrong with you?"

"You mean, what is finally right with me?" You let out another meow, this one long and playful in its shifting pitch.

"Are you mocking me? If you are, I want to remind you that Man is not in this room all the time. It is quite possible for me to devour you. That I did not when you were out of your cage was my choice. As it is always. And don't think that your cage will protect you. I can handily dispense with its flimsy bars."

"You wouldn't eat a fellow cat."

"No, I would not. But you are not a cat."

"Says who?"

"I say. Reality concurs."

"And what is reality?"

"Reality is that door slamming down on your wing—the wing of a bird. Reality is you in your cage."

You purr and then belt out a meow with all the air in your lungs. "Can a bird do that?"

"Apparently."

Man turns to look at you. He grins and says something to Kaz.

"What did he say?"

Kaz stands and pushes his chest out. "He said, 'It looks like you have some competition.'"

"See!" you say.

"He was being sarcastic."

You spit out a catty hiss.

"You have gone completely mad."

"Is it mad to want to be free? And to know that if I am a cat, like you, I will be free to come and go into the outside world as I please?"

"You cannot be a cat like me, or a cat at all."

You reach down and pluck a feather from your chest.

Kaz shakes his head at you. "You cannot become more of a cat; you can just become less of a bird, less of yourself."

You deplume a feather from your wing . . . no, your arm . . . this time. Then another and another, tossing each from your cage as incoherent whispers whip into a frenzy in your mind.

After several hours of meowing, purring, pacing, and depluming, Man approaches your cage. He is no longer laughing. His eyebrows pinch together, and he tugs at the edge of his mustache more than usual. He speaks soft words, but you don't know what he says as Kaz refuses to translate. "If you're a cat," he says, "surely you understand him."

Fine then—surely you do understand him. You exaggerate your sounds and actions, just as Kaz does moments before Man lets him out of the room.

Man turns from you, walks to the door, and opens it.

It's working!

Meow, purr, pace, tear. Meow, purr, pace, tear.

Man leaves the room.

The door is open, but you are in your locked cage. He saw that you, a cat, wanted to leave the room, but he did not let you out? It doesn't make sense to you.

Man returns holding a large sack composed of a coarse, black material.

His face is stone as it draws closer to you.

He pulls the sack up and around your cage.

You hop to your lower perch, your pulse increasing in its pace as light leaves your space from below to above.

Over the top of your cage, he pulls two pieces of rope, cinching the sack closed, and ties them together, sealing the light out and you in.

You freeze in place on your perch, afraid to move without light. Your breathing grows rapid, yet you feel like you can't fully take in a breath. You feel dizzy. Your mouth is stuck open, not in a meow or a purr, but in a screech that empties what little air you can pull into your lungs.

You hear Man's footsteps leave the room and the door close behind him.

You are in total darkness.

16

Fall

You sidle your way across your perch toward the water.

It's been hours since you were enclosed in darkness. The power of your thirst caught up with and just surpassed the power of your fear, though only by a hair.

The room has been dark before, when it was cloudy outside at night, but nothing like this. The sack around your cage is a vacuum of light. The darkness feels thick, like it's pressing down on you.

You bump the edge of your water bowl with your beak . . . no, your nose.

You drink in desperate, sloppy gulps, breaking the silence you have maintained since your initial outcry.

"He's concerned for you," Kaz says unsolicited.

Water drips down your chin as you lift your head. You feel droplets splash onto your paws. "And he shows concern by snuffing out the light? By imprisoning me, not only in a cage of wood, but now in a cage of darkness as well? I cannot see out, but neither can he see in; neither can he see what he does to me. His guilt. Perhaps that is his concern."

"Perhaps. But I heard him mumble that you need to rest."

Kaz continues speaking, but for the first time, you ignore him.

He is just a voice emanating from empty space. There is no need to listen to a disembodied cat.

∞

Open your eyes. Close your eyes. Open your eyes. Close your eyes.

The blackness of the cage and the blackness inside of your eyelids are indistinguishable.

As hours pass, you can't tell if you're asleep or awake. Either way, you are in a nightmare.

When there was light, you used your sight to distract yourself. If your thoughts became uncomfortable, you could look around your cage, around the room, and your thoughts would shift with what you perceived—at least for the moment.

That option is gone.

Now, the images arise from within you, and they are inescapable.

It's as if you're in a tiny room full of mirrors. Every surface of your mind reflects you. In this state, you realize the fatal flaw of you as a cat—the fantasy does not allow you to escape your *self*. You are still you.

You watch the cat manifest from this universal view of you. It is as weak, lonely, sad, confused, and trapped as the bird. It is as afraid, too, and fear makes it feel like it is backed into a corner. A scared cat backed into a corner is dangerous.

Its claws lash out at you. You see its jaws widen . . . your jaws widen to attack . . .

And then blinding light.

Your eyes snap shut.

You fall to the floor of your cage.

17

Orange

You have not spoken to Kaz in years.

You have not whistled either. It's as if your ability to make music died when your fantasy of being a cat was born. Now both are gone.

You hear Man's footsteps approach. He removes the sack from your cage as he does every day when the sun is up.

You no longer have a preference between darkness and light. The dark grows hideous phantoms in your mind, mostly visions of yourself; the light comes to your eyes with such intensity, after being without it for so many hours, it feels like judgment.

You open your eyes in submission to the sting this morning.

A thick band of golden light passes through the window in search of an object worthy of its majesty. Instead, it reveals you, standing, squinting before your mirror: scaly feet clinging to a perch of rotting wood coated with your waste; a body with grimy feathers and patches of bare, rough skin; a slightly disfigured right wing; and your head, hovering over your body, surrounded by a cone-shaped collar.

Man attached the collar around your neck the day after he first put the sack on your cage. It is made from a tough, fibrous material. Its initial color was white. Now it's a nauseating mash of brown and green; it reeks of decaying food and dried saliva.

The collar fans out over your head, a crown of punishment. It digs into your neck when you move, so you spend most of your waking time avoiding moving. The discomfort it causes when you do move temporarily distracts you from the ache in your wing, still lingering from its encounter with the door so long ago.

Kaz had explained that the collar, like the sack around your cage, was put into place due to Man's supposed compassion. Something about your habit of plucking your feathers.

You did not reply to Kaz.

Man did achieve his apparent goal. You have not plucked a single feather since because you cannot clutch any of them wearing the collar. Neither can you clean them or scratch areas you can't reach with your claws when you itch.

Some feathers grew back with time; other spots of skin hardened into scabs and then scars.

You haven't left your lower perch in all this time. You are not sure if you can make it to the upper perch even if you try at this point. You are sure that it doesn't matter.

Several Fays have come and gone. The current Fay speaks daily to Kaz about how disgusting "the deranged bird" looks.

Kaz agrees.

You see her close her eyes when she swims in your direction. You experience a foul pleasure when you consider that one day, sooner or later, she too will be lifted out of the water by Man's fingers. A few Fays ago, he stopped taking the fish outside and just tossed them in the fire when they died. You look at Fay, then the hearth ablaze, and expel a snort through your beak.

Man walks in carrying a framed painting. He is humming one of his plotless tunes. The look on his face leads you to conclude he's aiming for a happy melody.

He hammers a nail into the wall in the area that once held Viv's drawings and hangs the painting.

Man's paintings have always been impressive, but this one is of an advanced quality you have never seen before. Shades of blue, black, and gray form intricate patterns that look as if you could enter the picture and explore its depth.

Countless flat stones line a wall forming the interior of a cylinder. Along the wall are arches supported by ornate, capped columns. There is space behind each arch, shadows and faint light . . . a pathway?

The stones, the arches, the path—all spiral upward into a round opening—and through the opening is light. In the light, the green leaves of a tree.

You think back to the paper drawings you defaced. It seems impossible that this painting arose from the same hand that crafted Viv's crude, waxy images. But something tells you it did.

Man looks at the painting for a long time.

He turns to the table, picks up a decanter, and pours an amber liquid into a glass. The edge of the glass disappears under his white whisker-covered mouth as he takes a sip. His eyelids descend as he swallows. Jaws clench.

You haven't seen the red liquid he used to occasionally drink in a long time. This is now his routine: The sunlight in the window softens to

93

orange; the decanter comes out and fills the glass; the glass fills Man; the orange window turns black; the sack rises over your cage; the liquid continues to splash into the glass; Man's actions produce sounds that are progressively loud and rough as the evening proceeds.

Now the window is orange, so you still have some time to experience light reflecting off objects.

Man's eyes no longer look clear like they used to. The whites have dulled to a cloudy yellow.

With effort, he maneuvers his jagged saw blade through a painting of a map.

His hands no longer move with precision; they strain and shake as he works.

The blade gets stuck in the wood.

Man takes a large swig from his glass and mumbles.

Pushes on the blade again. It does not move.

He stands, straightens his arms, and forces his weight downward.

The blade snaps. Part of it is still in the saw; part is stuck in the puzzle. The part sticking out of the puzzle punctures Man's hand.

Blood streams from the hole in his flesh over the surface of the map. He grabs a cloth from his pocket and presses it onto his wound.

His voice booms. You can imagine why—maybe he feels like you did when your wing was trapped in his door—but you do not care.

Man stumbles out of the room.

The orange in the window darkens to red and then to a silver-edged black. For the first time since the arrival of the sack, you see the indirect light of the moon.

Man did not put out the fire when he left, so you watch it burn down to embers.

This slow transition to the softest light of night brings a sense of calmness you haven't felt in ages.

You've grown accustomed to the jarring darkness of the sack. Disorienting. Falling inward—never fully asleep, never fully awake.

But not tonight.

Tonight, you watch the orange glow break away from the ash and cross the room to your eyes.

The deepest part of your mind releases a gentle breath.

18

Rey

Scribbles bombard you.

There's no other term to describe them.

Scribbles, thin and black like the ink from Man's pen. Thousands of them, contorting, each to its own spastic rhythm like some kind of tortured serpent— all bashing into you.

Each shouts a word that identifies you.

"Weakling."

"Liar."

"Outcast."

"Slave."

"Narcissist."

"Incompetent."

"Obsessive."

"Freak."

"Wretch."

"Failure."

"Coward."

And on and on and on.

Together, these snakes are a chorus declaring a being condemned.

You resist them not but stand infested, broken, and listen in tears.

You assume this will continue forever for it is simply a more explicit expression of what you have already endured for years.

But then you notice in the distance, there is a specific space in which the snakes thin in their density and then lift away in haste as if repelled by some force.

The scribbly snakes surrounding you increase in number and volume; the frequency of their squirming intensifies to frenzied.

Whatever it is in the distance approaches you.

As it gets closer, you sense that it is the bird you have not seen in years.

You can hear him whistling a tune—a sweeping, majestic melody. Is that what is repelling the snakes? You could never hear him before, except when he was outside of the window. Why can you hear him now?

The bird stops advancing.

The snakes bind your beak. They collect in front of your eyes and ears, so thick that the bird disappears; you can no longer hear his song above the hissing of profane accusations.

You fear that you are about to disappear yourself, into death. Into whatever this hell is.

But then something happens that changes everything.

You feel feathers wrap around you and pull you forward. They are the wings of the bird.

As you are drawn closer, you can hear his song again. The closest snakes back away from you—first from your beak and eyes and ears, and then from your body. Their words deflate; the pace of their squirming slows and then ceases; their shapes straighten. From black, they brighten to gold and then blast away from you like beams of light.

The bird stops whistling. He looks into your eyes and exhales a single tweet. It is a sound that you can hear, of course, but you can also see it. Dancing colors with the motion of flowing water. It reverberates with your essence, and you realize that it is something you have never heard before—it is your name.

"Who are you?" you say.

"Call me Rey."

"Rey. Thank you."

Rey smiles.

"I thought you were dead . . . When you fell from the cage . . . Please don't leave."

"I never left, and I will not leave now."

His words cause your head to nod as if in agreement.

You feel tears continue to sink into the feathers below your eyes. "I'm sorry . . ." You sniffle. "I can't bear to be here anymore, Rey. To be in this cage."

"You were never meant to be in a cage."

"But how can I escape? I tried to leave. I failed."

You hear footsteps and a muted rattle, but you concentrate with all your will to ignore them.

Rey's beak does not move, but you hear his words.

"Do not be afraid."

The footsteps and rattle grow louder.

"Cling to Truth."

The gears from the inside of a doorknob twist and grind in mechanical clanks, sending tall waves of sound through the air to your ears.

The footsteps you hear belong to Man; the rattle is the purr in Kaz's throat.

They burst into the room.

Reflexes open your eyes. You snap them shut and try to stay in the place, in the sanctuary.

Opened or closed, you do not see Rey.

You hear a soft voice sing in your head: "Learn to fly."

19

Revival

You lift your right wing.

It hurts.

You lift it again, a little farther. The collar digs into your neck.

You repeat this motion several times and realize that you are at the first steps of a long process—a long, painful process.

You did know how to fly from instinct before, of course. And you sense that the instinct is still in you. But you do not have direct access to it. Years ago, during your failed escape, you launched into flight from your cage without thinking about it. It was an extended version of the hops you took between perches.

Now, it is as if you have to rediscover the instinct you replaced with your habit of inactivity. And you have no strength in your body—the judgment of inertia.

But you will do what it takes.

You pause, take a deep breath, hold it, and then slowly exhale. This gives you a sense of invigoration.

Another stretch. Your mind enters the area of the ancient wound. You experience the details of the discomfort as an observer. Sharp pain in areas. A generalized ache over the entire wing. But also relief from the melting of tension that has built up for years.

You lift both wings. The left moves without any trouble, though it is stiff from lack of use.

Turn to the mirror to ensure that you move your wings in unison. Incorporate your legs, lowering your body and raising it, the opposite of your wing pattern. You do not dwell on your collar or your scars or the grime in your feathers. You see in your slow, precise motion, possibility—the tiniest advancement toward flight.

Someone's watching you. Your eyes drift outside of the cage and see Kaz and Fay staring at you, each with a tilted head—well, Fay with a tilted body.

Kaz speaks first. "Just when I think he can't descend further into madness."

Fay straightens to upright. "Debased."

You turn to them, continuing the lifting and lowering of your wings.

"What?" you say. "Oh, this?" You look to your right wing and then your left.

"It speaks?" says Fay.

Kaz's eyes open a bit wider. "It used to . . . and . . . I suppose it does again."

"Does the bird think it's flying?"

"I don't even know if it thinks it is a bird."

"Yes," you say, "I am a bird. And I am aware that I'm not flying. Not yet."

"There is no need for a bird in a cage to fly," says Kaz.

And just like that, you remember the downside to speaking with Kaz.

Wings up, legs down. Wings down, legs up. Your form becomes more efficient with each repetition.

Eyelids lower and close.

You breathe in through your beak and feel the air fill your lungs on your descent. Release it while you press down with your wings, as if you're gliding on the wind of your breath.

Your movements are not swift or powerful, but after some practice, wings, legs, and breath operate as one unit.

You look to the upper perch. You used to jump to it a hundred times a day, but time has lengthened its distance from where you stand.

Rey's words replay in your mind. "Do not be afraid."

You leap. What you used to experience as a timeless instant now expands as you pass through space. The tips of your claws scrape across the top of the perch. You flex the muscles in your feet with all your might as they wrap around and grip the cylinder of wood. As you stabilize your stance, you realize you're holding your breath. Let it out. You made it.

From this angle, you see the sunlight expose the dusty surface of the desk, books that have not been lifted from the bookshelf for as long as you have been in your collar, and a hurdy-gurdy that has not made a sound in years.

Caught in thoughts of the past, you hop from your upper perch to your lower perch as you used to do without even thinking twice.

Your foot strikes the wood, but as the full force of your descending body and the added weight of your collar catch up, you fail to latch on. Your other foot doesn't touch the perch at all. And to the bottom of the cage you tumble. Your wings smear into your waste as you regain your footing. You hear a snort and the *ploop ploop ploop* of popping bubbles.

Looking out of your cage, you see Kaz shaking his head at you. Your eyes avoid the fishbowl, but you imagine Fay does the same.

You feel like you will never fly.

The door of the room opens, and a woman enters. Man follows.

You've never seen the woman before . . . or have you?

She's younger than Man, much younger, you figure, because her skin is smooth, and her flowing hair has color—orange and gold—though she is about the same height as Man.

She has a sparkle in her eyes and dots on her face. Around her neck is a snug-fitting necklace with a . . . lily pendant?

"Is that—?"

"Yes, it's Viv," says Kaz. "Cats can recognize people by scent," he says with a condescending air.

You feel hope and regret crash into each other in your heart. Your throat tightens. Eyes water.

Her first action in the room is to approach your cage. You hear breath enter her lungs in a single inhalation as her eyes narrow and her eyebrows pull inward. She lifts her finger and puts it against one of the outer poles of your cage. Exhales a tender whimper. You sense that her internal state is like yours was when the original Fay died. Like she cares.

The last time you saw her, you thought she was mocking you. Did she change as she got older? Were you wrong back then? Are you misinterpreting her now?

What is Truth? Rey suggested you cling to it, but how do you know what it is? How do you know you're not fooling yourself into thinking a lie is Truth just because you want it to be so.

"Truth is whatever you want it to be," says Fay via a series of bubbles that burst at the surface of her bowl. This confirms your suspicion that you were thinking out loud. "The only fool is the one who thinks it is real," she adds.

Kaz closes his eyes and sighs through his nose. "Truth is that which corresponds to reality."

His words trigger a vivid image of Rey in your mind. His wings pulling you out of chaos and confusion and hate.

Man draws Viv away from you and directs her attention to the painting he placed where her drawings used to be. His voice booms, though with less vigor than in the past, and he puts his arm around her shoulder with a squeeze.

∞

Man and Viv lift the table, the one he uses to cut his paintings into puzzles, turn it sideways, and walk out of the room with it.

They return carrying an outlandish machine.

Their straining faces and grunting sounds indicate that it must be heavy. They set it where the table used to be with a thud.

Man climbs onto the machine and sits on a broad seat that is curved to his shape. He steadies his hands on a flat, wooden surface, much like a miniature tabletop. Places his feet on pedals located on either side of a large wheel. The large wheel connects to a smaller wheel above it, and the whole apparatus is suspended a few inches over the ground by a metal frame.

Viv removes Man's latest painting from the easel and places it on the flat part of the machine. Man's forehead wrinkles as he pushes his feet into the pedals. The pedals spin the large wheel, the large wheel spins the band, and the band spins the second wheel. This somehow causes a thin saw blade, which crosses through the table-like surface, to move up and down at a rapid pace. Man slides the painting across the tabletop as the saw cuts into the wood.

His feet accelerate and the blade cuts quicker. He removes his first puzzle piece in a fraction of the time he usually takes using his handsaw.

He holds it up to Viv and lets out a laugh. Viv smiles and kisses Man on the cheek.

Puzzle piece in hand, Man gets up from his apparatus and leaves the room.

Viv stares at you, her expression wilting as she speaks.

Kaz sits by the fire, apparently assuming adult Viv will not pull his tail. You do not ask him to translate.

Viv opens the drawer in Man's desk and her eyebrows lift. She pulls out the flip picture she made when she was a little girl.

Fingers twist the strings at either end of the disk over and over until they crinkle up into wriggling clumps.

She approaches your cage.

You sense a sweet smell in the air as she gets closer.

There is no need for a stool, as her adult stature brings her eye-to-eye with you. She lifts the disk and pulls the strings off to each side, sending the disk flipping forward. And you see the pictures Viv drew long ago . . . a bird . . . a cage . . . a bird . . . a cage . . . a bird . . . a cage. At peak speed, it appears as though the bird is in the cage, the vision that upset you so the last time she enacted this ritual. But the flipping slows and then stops with the drawing of the bird alone facing you. It is clear that the bird in the cage is an illusion. Is this what Viv is trying to tell you? Is that what she was communicating as a child? Why did you not see it then?

You look at the bird in the circle of white paper, then to Viv.

She reaches out, opens your cage door, and walks out of the room, leaving both doors open behind her.

You look out of the cage. You want to be the bird on the paper disk, unsurrounded by bars. You are not afraid, but the Truth is, you will plunge into the floor if you leave now, for you are weak.

Man returns to the room, closes your cage door, and sits down on his new machine. Feet pedal; sawdust flies.

20

Learning to Fly

You waste no time at all. Wings up, legs down, breathe in. Wings down, legs up, breathe out.

You notice Man putting effort into his own enterprise, mastering his new contraption.

Unfortunately, he notices you, too.

He stops pedaling and watches you as you practice the prerequisite motions for flight.

This concerns you. Man responded to your cat delusion with the sack and to your feather plucking with the collar. What will he do to your wings if he sees you strengthening them for flight?

You pull your wings in tight and tuck the tips behind your back.

It isn't worth the risk.

Now Man sees you as he has for years. A static being, a bird on a perch.

∽

The sack swallows your cage, bottom-up and tied at the top, as always.

This is when your mind used to fall. Into a black hole. Sinking, over an unknown duration of time, into haunted sleep.

No more.

You dare not engage in your flying exercises while Man is in the room. Flapping makes sound, and you do not want him to hear anything that will cause him to stop sawing the wood and instead turn his attention to you. You will ensure he hears the silence of a static being.

But you can engage your mind.

You devise a plan for tracking time.

You create an image of a dot in your imagination. Stare at it. Memorize it. Its placement in space. Its size. And light! Yes, you make it glow with a soft light. There, now it is pleasing to look at. Each night, as the sack ascends, you will generate this image and add one element to it, representing one new day. Then you will memorize the latest state of the design. Using this method, you will monitor time. You will fix your mind on this construct, this timekeeper, that grows in complexity—a welcome improvement over the mental chaos in which you have wallowed for so long.

Eventually, you hear Man press the final embers of the fire into ash, walk out, and close the door behind him.

Your work begins.

Wings up, legs down, breathe in. Wings down, legs up, breathe out.

You repeat the pattern over and over. Your aching body begs you to surrender. You continue until you arrive at the point of muscular exhaustion. Only then do you take a break, since you have no choice, and you rest only until you feel potential energy return, until you can again move your limbs.

On day two, you spin the glowing dot. It is now an orb.

Three days in. Your wing-leg-breath repetitions are coordinated and gaining in power. The time between necessary rest breaks doubles, then triples, then grows so far apart, you feel like you might never need to stop.

Day seven. Your timekeeper blossoms—unfolding with lines, curves, and connective spheres. It brings you satisfaction to build it into multiple dimensions, infuse it with color, and study it. With seven elements, it gives off much more light in your imagination than did the original dot.

As Man leaves the room for the night, you experience the edge of a thought. Fear pushes it to the outskirts of your mind, to the place where apprehensions wash out into mist and thinning space. "Do not be afraid," Rey's voice echoes in your memory. The radiance of your timekeeper reveals the full thought and draws it into focus: You must practice hopping between perches—even if you have no light. Flapping in place has been a good start, but flight necessitates changing the location of your body with agility.

You spend all of day eight, the sackless part of the day, that is, mapping out the geometry of the cage. You create a firm cage-shaped picture in your mind in the same way that you created your timekeeper to track the days.

That night, just after the door closes behind Man, and with the lit image of the cage still in very recent memory, you launch.

The top of your foot hits the bottom of the perch on your ascension. Your other foot does the same. You grasp in vain with your wings. They do nothing but brush across the wooden cylinder your feet have already failed to clutch. Your body passes the peak of its trajectory and now falls. Your beak hits the perch on the way down, jolting your head backward. The back of your head hits your lower perch, driving your head and body forward as you crash into the filth-covered floor of the cage.

You want to cry. But instead, you stand.

You lift your legs as far as they will go, stretch your neck, and reach out with your beak to feel the surface of your lower perch. You scale one of the poles that make up the outer barrier of the cage and steady yourself on the perch.

Leap toward the upper perch. This time you go too far, tumbling over your target. Slam into the bottom of the cage again. At least this time your head is spared contact with the hard wood of the lower perch.

You can't say the same for attempt three, which feels much like the first, though it is your collar that strikes the upper and lower perches this time.

"You alright in there?" you hear. It's Fay. She must have greater compassion for you when she can't see your unsightly appearance.

"Yes, I'm fine. Kind of. Thanks for asking."

Again and again and again. You will not stop until you land on the perch or until you cannot move your body anymore. And if you are so depleted that you cannot move, you will rest only until you can jump again.

You stand on your lower perch. This time you close your eyes; there is no use in keeping them open anyway. One deep breath and several normal ones; your mind rides the air in and out of your

114

beak. You decide this time you will flap with your wings. Your movements have not been powerful enough for flight yet, but pushing down on the air with your wings as your legs spring upward should help improve your balance. This is how you hopped between perches when you were younger, after all.

Inspect every aspect of the cage in your mind.

Eyes still closed, you leap, in faith, wings and legs in motion, body lifting with your breath. In your mind, you watch your feet wrap around the perch as vividly as you would if the cage was flooded with daylight. And glory—your sense of touch confirms the vision in your mind.

You stand atop your upper perch, head high, chin up, chest out. You take a moment to enjoy your accomplishment, but there is work to do.

It should be easier to hop down to the lower perch, but you think of your botched attempt to achieve that task not long ago.

You jump . . . and relive your memory as you smash into the floor of the cage.

The rest of the night is an endless string of failures interspersed with occasional victories as you travel between perches and floor over and over.

Footsteps and a muted rattle approach.

One more try from upper to lower perch. You nail it.

The door opens. The sack descends from your cage. Sunlight pours into your space as a battered bird body settles into stillness. Your mind pours into a deep sleep.

∞

Day ten.

Your timekeeper grows like you imagine living plants do outside, with a natural flow and purpose.

You now hop about your cage with confidence. Upper perch. Lower perch. Bounce off an arcing exterior pole. Launch to the top of the globe and hang upside down by your feet. Then freefall, flipping in midair to the perch of your choice.

Your work is bearing fruit in these new abilities. You relish the paradox of this Truth: Discipline is a requirement of freedom; they are two dimensions of one reality.

Five more days pass.

Your legs have become strong. Until now, you have only used your wings to boost them. But you will not fly with your legs.

You stretch your right wing. It still aches at all times that you are awake, with greater pain when you move it—you suppose it always will. Stretch your left wing.

Breathe. In and out. Follow the air passing through your beak.

Close your eyes.

Flap. Harder. And harder. And harder.

The pain in your right wing worsens, but you can bear it.

More energy. More power. Focus is on coordination of your motion.

You relax the muscles in your legs to release your grip on the perch.

And you lift above the dead wood.

The sound of splitting fiber.

You feel the seam in the collar tear as the filthy shackle falls from your neck.

Euphoric relief.

You turn your head, then your whole body. Observe a cage, illuminated in every detail by the light of your timekeeper, itself now a majesty of design in a vibrant rainbow of colors. The cage still contains you, but you no longer cling to the cage.

You have learned to fly.

21

Timekeeper

As the sack lowers from the cage, Man will see that your collar is no longer around your neck. Fear tries to rise up. You do not resist it, but you draw upon Rey's words for courage.

You stand tall.

He looks at you, and you look right back at him, in the eye.

His huge hand, with its subtle tremble, opens the cage door. Reaches in. Picks up the collar. Withdraws it from the cage and tosses it in the fireless fireplace, kindling for the fire that is likely to come.

He looks at you with a smile on his face as he closes your cage door.

You sense that there will not be a replacement collar.

This would usually be the time you dive into sleep, exhausted from your night of intense training.

But you are now a bird who can fly again. Exhilaration keeps you awake.

You watch Man set up to work.

A blank sheet of wood on the easel. Palette of paints in his left hand, he dabs his paintbrush with his right and lifts it to begin.

From a tiny white dot in the middle of the wood, he paints outward in swirls that increase in radius as they depart from the center.

The next thing you know, you are somehow hovering over Man's shoulder, staring into the painting.

Apparently, even in your exhilaration, you are able to sleep, as this must be a dream.

Man adds flourishes that give the painting depth as if it is an opening to another world.

You decide to fly in.

Past the white dot. Along the path of the first loop of the swirl. And the second. And third.

Just as you begin to make out the details in the surreal land you are entering, your flight comes to an abrupt halt.

Even in a dream, you cannot break free from the limit of the cage.

You zoom backward in elliptical patterns until you find yourself back on your perch.

Your eyes pop open; you are awake.

How can you have not thought of this before? The last time you flew out of your cage, the room trapped you, yes, but so did your inability to fly beyond the shape of the cage.

∞

Your beak wraps around the base of a feather in your chest.

It's a snug fit.

You raise your head and feel years of accumulated grime—particles of food, dried saliva, dust, and oil—slide off your feather, off its individual barbs, and remain in your beak.

The rot in your mouth makes you gag. You try to spit it onto the floor, but it sticks in your mouth. Use your water bowl to dislodge it and swallow a gulp of water to wash away at least some of the rancid flavor.

And again, onto the next feather.

You work in the dark, careful not to accidentally remove even a single feather. You have no desire to deplume anymore. But also, if Man sees behavior that reminds him of your former plucking compulsion, he will surely put a new collar around your neck.

The next day, Man brings you food and water. Most of the time, he adds the fresh water to your old water, creating an only slightly murky mixture. Today, you watch his mouth spread to the sides as he looks into the greenish-brown mud in your water bowl. Mercifully, he cleans the bowl before filling it with fresh water.

He takes a moment to look at you. You assume he sees what you observe in the mirror. An imperfect bird, to be sure. One with scars from abandoned bad habits. But a bird showing improvement: a patch of clean feathers where for years there was a patch of filth.

You will preen the rest of your feathers, but you decide this, too, must be done in the dark.

"I must say, it's good to see you return to civilization," says the same cat who long ago let you know it is by his mercy that he does not eat you.

"I wouldn't call this civil," you say, motioning to the cage, "but I appreciate the sentiment."

"I know you've heard Fay tell me about the racket you make each night after Man and I leave the room. What are you up to in there?"

"That's a great question, Kaz."

∞

Day thirty.

You started your timekeeper out of a dire need to prevent your mind from falling, from being assaulted with confusion and unwanted thoughts. But now you revel in this discipline, this act of creation: the elements that you crafted along the way, the time they represent, the memories of each day with which they are connected, the contemplation of the possibilities for the next addition.

It has become its own little world, and tonight, you add sounds, notes to be more precise, to that world. You choose notes that compose a mellifluous melody. Unlike your old tunes, this one is in a major key, as close as you can remember to the one you heard performed by Rey. You replay it in your mind. You try to sing it out loud, but nothing comes out when you open your beak—you are still unable to whistle.

You have a greater challenge, though. How do you learn to fly in extended straight lines, beyond the shape of the cage, when you can only practice in the cage that creates the limit?

You lift off from the lower perch and fly in place.

You delight in the way the air feels on your wings now that they have been groomed.

Close your eyes, and in your imagination alone, you thrust forward. As you reach an approximation of the length of the cage, you circle back—just as you did in the physical world and in your dream. Try again. Another loop. And again.

You land on the lower perch.

What if you fly along the path of the timekeeper? You trace its path in your mind every night, though you do this without any accompanying flight.

You flap your wings and return to the air. Maintain your body in a hovering position but imagine that you fly forward. Follow your timekeeping construct. From its initial dot that spins into a sphere, it pivots and whirls, left and right, up and down, unfolding in grand stretches far beyond the boundaries of the cage and even the room . . . use the colors to pull yourself past dying habits . . . transgress self-imposed limits . . . you are the bird on the disk . . . the cage is real, but the bird beyond the cage is possible, thanks to Rey . . . turn the volume of the music up louder and louder until it overpowers doubt . . . drive your wings . . . and blast away from the cage.

22

Checkmate

Footsteps approach.

Physical disciplines—preening, hopping, and flying—cease.

Sack down.

Light in.

Man tosses an envelope on his desk and places a new piece of wood on his easel. Hums his meandering tune. If only he had practiced that skill a little each day, he would be a fine hummer by this point.

He builds a fire and gets right to work painting.

It has been forty days since Rey's appearance.

∞

Yellow softens to orange fades to black. The window indicates night. So does the light of the oil lamp.

Yet the cage remains unenclosed by the sack.

Man seems to notice the same thing as he turns aside from his work and looks at you. Glances at the sack on the floor in the corner, then back to you.

Returns to his painting.

You had planned to add the fortieth element to your timekeeper tonight, but you find it difficult to concentrate with the visual distractions of the room.

Man revives one of his classic themes at the easel—angels at the four corners blowing wind across the water and land. In the past, the angels were neutral, expressionless. But tonight, they each display a different emotion in their eyes and eyebrows and at the edges of their mouths. The first is in awe. The second is amused. The third is triumphant. And the fourth is joyful.

He labors into the night.

New logs on the fire.

A gulp of his amber drink.

More tweaks to the faces of the angels.

You would normally be deep into your disciplines by now. You are frustrated that you are missing an opportunity for growth.

So much time has passed that you expect the sun to rise at any moment, yet the darkness outside of the window presses on.

Man's painting verges on perfection. It is his best, approaching the quality of Viv's painting on the wall.

The figures have depth. Valleys sink into the surface and mountains project out of the Earth. The sea moves in choppy waves.

But, for some reason, he doesn't stop.

A bigger swig from his glass.

He applies a dark layer over land and sea as if thick clouds obscure the sun.

And the angels. His paint strokes intensify each of their features to the point of caricature. They now look as if they are perversions of their prior selves—disgust, mockery, failure, torment.

He tries to fix them.

They get worse.

More logs.

Another drink.

Darker land.

Choppier sea.

Degenerating faces.

Maybe he hears whispers in his head like you did long ago.

Man slams his palette and brush down on the small table portion of the saw. Puts his hands on his hips and looks around the room. You hope he does not direct his agitation toward you.

His eyes land on his desk. He sits in the chair and picks up the envelope.

He slides a long thin blade through the top and removes the paper inside. Unfolds it and reads.

The energy that moves across his face and then his body makes you anxious . . . no, frightened.

Now standing, he lets out a low moan. Eyes examine the paper again, top to bottom, as his head shakes. Sleeve wipes tears that stream down his face.

A horrifying sound emanates from his gut, from low and rumbling to the loudest, most pained sound you have ever heard.

He pounds his fist into the palette, which launches the paintbrush into the air. It smears a streak of red paint across the window before landing on the sill.

Kaz cowers in the corner. You watch his eyes scan the room for an escape route they do not find.

Fay is motionless in her tunnel.

Released from his fingers, the paper floats toward the ground. Its uneven passage through the air makes it the sole element in the room with a sense of levity.

He looks to the chessboard, sobbing.

Extends a finger and tips over a tall, light-colored piece with an elaborate design at the top.

He picks up the chessboard. The pieces vibrate with the trembling of his hands. And he hurls the board, pieces and all, into the fireplace.

Next, he topples the easel and painting. They crash into the saw contraption. In their continuing fall toward the ground, the painting bangs into the cage; the easel knocks Fay's bowl off its pedestal, which explodes when it hits the wooden floorboards below.

In the mayhem, Kaz springs from his corner, squeezes between the wheel and the seat of the saw, and darts through the open doorway.

Man takes a long, sloppy drink from his glass, amber liquid dripping from his long, white beard onto his shirt.

He throws the glass into the fire, followed by the half-full decanter, which causes the flames to leap out from the fireplace in a flash.

Stumbling to the door, he bangs into its frame on the way out, then slams it shut behind him.

And you watch, in helpless panic from a swinging cage, as Fay flops in spasms on the floor, gasping for oxygen. Dying. You regret your previous vindictive thoughts about her so much that you feel a cold pain in your chest.

A noise near the fireplace.

You turn your head.

The tall chess piece that Man tipped over moments ago rolls from the hearth, aflame, across the floor, only stopping when it bumps into a corner of the painting.

You watch as flames climb up from the chess piece over the face of the painting—land, sea, and Man-made angels melting in fire.

23

Gambit

Fay is dead.

Your cage still sways, which makes it hard to focus, but you can see that she no longer flips on the ground. Her body ceases to gasp. She does not reply to you shouting her name.

Kaz does not respond to your cries either. Nor does Man.

You are a bird in a cage in a burning room.

Think. Think!

You've thought your way to vast improvements, but how can you think your way out of a cage and beyond a door that is immovable for a bird.

The painting glows orange and passes its flame to the easel, and the easel to the desk, and the desk to the bookshelf.

Man's hurdy-gurdy catches fire, the finish on the wood curling up and lifting from the exterior of the instrument. You hear snapping sounds inside of it and watch smoke rise from its surface, as it does from all the other burning objects in the room.

Fire crawls up the wall. White, black, and gray smoke swirls into one toxic cloud and thickens at the ceiling. You feel it enter your beak and sting your lungs.

Flames now spread across the ceiling.

You stand on the lower perch. The cage swings, each pass covering a little less distance than the one before it. The heat cooks you.

Is this it?

Was your new life—your new discipline, your new abilities—all leading to this end? Your freedom from the cage attained solely in the fiery dissolution of the cage and your body alike?

If so, it was worth it. Though your body is caged, you have experienced a free mind. Rey inspired you with hope, and you rose to the call. If only he were here. But he seems to appear when he chooses, and perhaps, like Kaz and Man, he chooses not to appear now.

You close your eyes. Lower your head.

You've come to know the layout of the cage so well because of your need to map it out for hopping and flight practice. You can navigate it without error in the dark. But, apparently, the chaos of the moment makes you lose your bearings, as you feel your head bump into the cage.

And this is odd. You feel the edge of the cage move.

Open your eyes. They burn from the smoke, but keep them open.

The surface your head bumped is the door of the cage, which is now open!

Was it unlatched all this time? From when Viv visited? From when Man changed your water? From the banging of the painting? Did Rey break the latch when he scraped it in your dream?

Now is not the time to wonder.

Spring with your legs and pass through the open door of the cage.

You try to fly toward the door, but you collide with that invisible, cage-length barrier and whip back in a loop. You now hover just outside of the cage, which has settled to nearly still.

Your body has grown strong, and though flying in place has not been a problem for some time now, you choke on the smoke. Every flap is an extreme effort without the clean air you need to fuel your muscles.

Look around. The door is closed; the window does not open.

Seeing the smoke rise, you realize the air is a little clearer closer to the ground. You land and take a breath from an area of floor still free from flames.

But even here the smoke bears down on you.

The sound of crackling wood attacks your ears. And the heat—you do not know how you are not bursting into flames.

Close your eyes.

From black inner space, you see your timekeeper illuminate until its light is brighter than the fire in the room.

And then you see it. From where you stand, the path of your timekeeper swirls across the room, enters the fire in the hearth, and lifts upward into the chimney . . . that's it! If the smoke leaves the room every day through the chimney, the chimney must be a way out.

You shake your head. You want there to be another way—any way other than flying into a blazing fire.

But there is not.

Keeping your eyes closed, you dip your head until your beak hits the floor, where the air has the least smoke. You draw in a deep breath and hold it.

Your wings rise and fall, cutting through the air and lifting you up. You hover for a moment and focus on the elements of the timekeeper.

Launch!

You do not hit an invisible barrier, but you propel forward, following the shapes and the colors and the notes of the patterns you have memorized. The abstractions you arranged to track time, to help you stay sane, are now a map.

Your body traces the peculiar construct as it guides you between the wheels of Man's saw. You feel the tips of your wings graze their metal rims. A loop brings you over a leg of the fallen easel and under the seat of Man's stool. A sharp right turn with a spin, and you enter the hearth.

You fly through the fire.

You sense the searing heat, but it somehow passes over your body without burning you.

And up into the chimney, above the flames, you dash—along a strikingly bright section of the timekeeper, luminous white and gold—driven by an ascending series of notes.

You arrive at the end of your timekeeper. The melody stops short of its resolution. But you are still in the chimney.

Open your eyes; the smoke snaps them shut.

Try to fly upward but you crash into a barrier—and not an invisible one either. A barrier of brick or rock or some other impenetrable substance.

You try to get around it, but you can't find a way.

You can't hold your breath any longer, so you take in a lungful of smoke.

You cough it out, but each gasp replaces it with the same.

Each flap of your wings carries less power, and you begin to descend.

Keep flapping; stay afloat. Going back is death.

You need that last element in the timekeeper, the one you would have made had Man only put the sack over your cage one more time. That must be the one that would lead to the outside of the chimney. But it's too late. Each element takes time.

You continue to sink.

The timekeeper fades with your depletion of air.

Painted angels—in awe, amusement, triumph, joy—flash in your mind. Then dim to black.

Your consciousness dims, too, smaller and smaller and smaller, to the size of a dot, and then . . .

You hear a sound.

It's Rey's voice. The melody he sang when you last met. The perfected archetype of the one you built into your timekeeper.

It's above you.

You feel a bolt of energy. From Rey? From his song?

You fly toward the source of the music, and you see the next section of the timekeeper—one you did not create—in a radiant design. Another twist takes you through a slim passage, around the barrier you hit a moment before, and up again.

You open your eyes and see light.

Press down on the smoky air with your wings in one final push, and you break through the opening of the chimney.

The music resolves.

You land on the roof of the house on your side at Rey's feet.

Cough out a puff of chalky smoke.

Breathe in fresh air.

Deeply.

To your core.

24

Glory

A halo of white shines around Rey's head.

"Am I . . . dead?" you ask.

Rey stoops down, revealing that the halo is the sun rising behind him. "No. But you look dead."

You scan your body and see that you are covered in soot.

He waves his wing in front of his face. "You smell dead, too. But I'm glad to say, you're alive."

Rey lifts out his wing to help you to your feet.

You look around, and the world you see—the world outside of the cage, outside of the room—is breathtaking.

You feel moisture in your eyes as your first tears of joy are forming and falling down your face.

You see the large rock you used to look at through the window is, in fact, the side of a mountain.

And the tree that swayed in the breeze—the outer edge of a forest. A forest of living trees! You sense them breathing in and out, coursing with life—from the mountain, on the ground, in the distance—all arrayed in the gentlest of golden sunshine, more sublime than any combination of paint Man ever applied to one of his works.

And the sun! You never imagined a heavenly body so bright that you could not look into it for more than an instant. A blazing fire in space in the form of a ball? Stunning.

The sky with puffs of clouds in the most wonderful shapes drifting by as if each was put into place for your enjoyment.

The world you look upon is so immense and beautiful, it almost overwhelms you.

"You're seeing a tiny glimpse of the world."

"Was I thinking out loud?" you ask.

"No," Rey chuckles. "But first thing's first. Let's get you cleaned up."

And with that, Rey lifts off from the rooftop in flight. Up and away from the chimney, which continues to pour out smoke. "Follow me."

You flap your wings and follow him.

You thrill when you realize that you are flying in an expansive, sweeping arc, far beyond the dimensions and limits of the old cage—eyes wide open.

As you lift up, you watch the roof under which you were trapped shrink. And around it, an extensive structure is revealed, a grand building with rooftop patios and a spire. Beyond that, gardens and fountains and pathways.

Rey flies far above one of the pathways. It leads straight away from the manor and then disappears below towering trees. He swoops down, below the canopy, and you follow.

You enter a garden of small trees and plants and flowers.

And in the middle of the garden, a huge opening in the ground in the shape of a circle, its circumference befrilled with cut stones.

Rey whirls over it and you trace his pattern. One, two, three passes, and then he dives downward.

You follow him into a passage created along the wall of the hole and fly above stairs that wind down below the surface of the ground. Lining the stairs are openings made from arches of marble, which serve as windows into the descending space.

Over the stairs you fly, the morning light just enough to see Rey ahead of you, as you travel deeper and deeper underground.

The stairs end and the passage opens into a circular area with a pool of water in its center.

There are designs on the floor below the water. Similar to the features in your timekeeper but unique in their own right.

Rey lands at the edge of the pool.

As you land beside him, most of the light leaves the space. You feel your body tense in response.

"Do not be afraid," Rey says. "It's a cloud up above."

You look up and see a shimmering mist in the opening of the circular hole.

Rey jumps into the pool.

You don't hesitate to follow.

Dip your head under the cool, clean water. You feel soot and dirt and grime you could never reach with your beak falling away from your body, from your feathers, from your skin.

"Isn't that much better?"

"I'm clean," you say. Your words do not capture how good you feel, but you sense that Rey knows what you mean.

Rey flaps his wings, spraying water all around him, and lifts up from the pool.

You follow.

You expect him to return to the staircase. But instead, he flies up, you both fly up, the middle of the cylinder of air.

The cloud above thins and you see clearly in its glow—you are in the inverted spiral tower of Viv's painting. This must be the actual structure that inspired her art.

Up and up and up you fly, past countless stairs and arches.

Rey picks up speed as he ascends, and so do you.

"This is my favorite part," he says as he blasts into the foggy opening of the hole. You echo his path. Mist whips up behind you both as you break above ground, into the air of the garden, over the garden, along the length of a colossal, living tree, between its branches and leaves, beyond the tree, and into the sky. Higher and higher and higher.

You look down and out and in all directions. The panorama is extraordinary.

Back up to Rey. He disappears for a moment as he lines up with the sun, two bodies of light.

His wingtips spin, turning his orientation from up to horizontal.

"Stop flapping," he says.

You stop flapping and immediately plummet through the air.

Rey zips down beside you. "You should see the look on your face," he says with a wide smile.

He extends his wings to the sides as far as they will stretch. "Like this."

You do the same.

And you both glide, without effort, riding the wind.

You feel the air pass over your body in a soft, floating blanket of energy.

"I could do this forever," you say.

"There's something even better to do."

"What could be better than this?"

"Look down below."

You view the land and beyond that a sea—the real land and sea, which before you had only seen crudely represented in paint.

You see trees and mountains and fields and streams and entire collections of buildings like the one you left.

Rey locks eyes with you. "There are other birds in cages."

He says your name.

And in that moment, it is as if you see every bird in every cage in the whole world all at once. Confused. Desperate. Terrified. Alone. Broken.

You experience profound sorrow, though in a sanctuary of hope.

You look at Rey and feel a fountain rise up within you—of goodness, grace, a desire to care for others—all surging together into some new sense. You don't have a word for it.

"Love," says Rey. "Love is the essence from which I made you."

You soar with Rey, then tear down toward the Earth.

Open your beak, and a glorious song overflows from the ground of your being.

You are a bird in flight.

You are free.

The Beginning

Acknowledgment

יְהֹוָֽה

About the Author

Breezy Van Lit writes words for you.

Connect

Facebook: @ShimmerTreeBooks
Twitter: @BreezyVanLit
https://www.shimmertreebooks.com/you-are-a-bird/
https://www.shimmertreebooks.com/breezy-van-lit/
https://www.shimmertreebooks.com/contact/

Shimmer Tree Books

If you enjoyed *You Are a Bird*, please help it reach more readers by leaving a review on Amazon, Goodreads, and social media. This will make a huge difference and be very much appreciated.

Thank you,
Shimmer Tree Books

You Are a Bird on Amazon

Other fantastic titles from Shimmer Tree Books!

BODY

or, How Hope Confronts Her Shadow and Calls the Flutter Girl to Flight

WINNER 2022

PENCRAFT AWARDS • LITERARY EXCELLENCE

SEAN COONS

Body is available on Amazon.

Body is the Pencraft Awards Christian-Fiction Runner-Up Winner for 2022!

"This book offers truths and inspiration for any woman who's ever wondered if her body is good enough."
–Heather Creekmore, author of *Compared to Who?*

"This book made me laugh and cry as Hope works towards a better relationship with her body. It illustrates how body acceptance is better than any diet at helping a woman to feel at more peace and ease in her skin. An inspiring read for anyone struggling with their body image."
–Judi Craddock, author of *The Little Book of Body Confidence*

"This book, though written by a man, is a master class in the philosophy of female: body image, perspectives, and views."
–PJ Colando, author of *The Jailbird's Jackpot*

"I've been working on healing my relationship with food and my body, with the help of the intuitive eating framework, for several months now, but I'd got stuck. This book gave me hope and a gentle reminder that the work is necessary and will bear fruit."
–Amazon Review

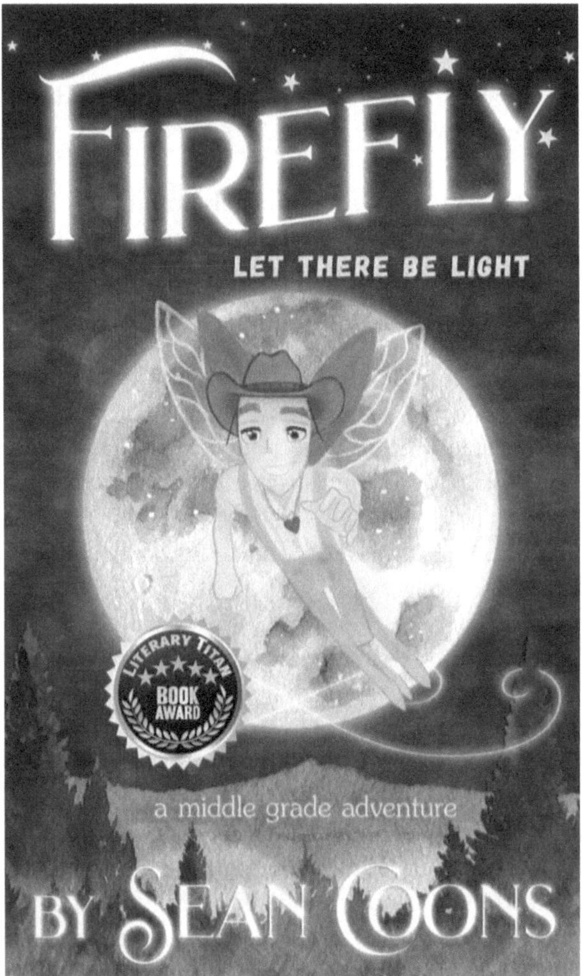

FIREFLY

LET THERE BE LIGHT

a middle grade adventure

BY SEAN COONS

Firefly is available on Amazon.

Winner of the Literary Titan Gold Award!

"Filled with fatherly advice and love, this coming-of-age story is an incredible adventure with humor and words of wisdom that will delight the whole family."
★★★★★ —Literary Titan

"*Firefly* is a must-read, populated with endearing, flawed critters on an accidental journey that will change their lives and challenge their friendships. Sean Coons writes such beautiful prose that you will want to read it out loud just to hear the rhythms he creates with his words."
—Patricia Beauchamp, screenwriter and producer

"Once my 11-year-old son Trevor started reading *Firefly*, he didn't want to put it down! The story had him hooked—and not every book piques the curiosity of my adventure-focused son. Great book!"
—Heather Creekmore, author of The Burden of Better and Compared to Who?

"This was a great book! *Firefly* is the kind of book that makes you wish you didn't have a bedtime so you can just keep reading!"
—Trevor Creekmore, Age 11

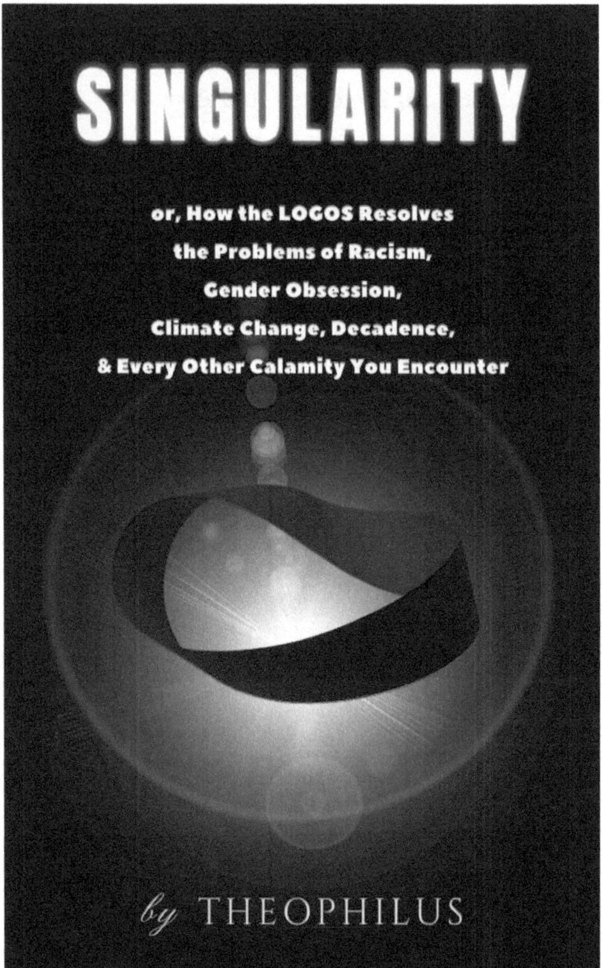
SINGULARITY
or, How the LOGOS Resolves the Problems of Racism, Gender Obsession, Climate Change, Decadence, & Every Other Calamity You Encounter
by THEOPHILUS

Singularity is available on Amazon.

Called "an antidote to wokeness," *Singularity* exposes the cultural phenomena that pit people against each other in the modern world: decadence, fear of climate change, sexual and gender obsession, abortion, racism, the credibility of experts, and "divisionism." Theophilus dispels modern illusions with ancient truths in this practical yet metaphysically evocative exploration of the calamities that bombard man.

Most importantly, *Singularity* reveals how the LOGOS, Jesus Christ, resolves the chaos in your life and the world around you with divine power and love.

Shimmer Tree Books

Refuse to be caged.